H. E. BA...

My Uncle Silas

➤➤◆➤➤

INTRODUCED BY
V. S. PRITCHETT

Oxford New York

OXFORD UNIVERSITY PRESS

Oxford University Press, Walton Street, Oxford OX2 6DP

London New York Toronto
Delhi Bombay Calcutta Madras Karachi
Kuala Lumpur Singapore Hong Kong Tokyo
Nairobi Dar es Salaam Cape Town
Melbourne Auckland

and associated companies in
Beirut Berlin Ibadan Mexico City Nicosia

Oxford is a trade mark of Oxford University Press

First published 1939 by Jonathan Cape
First issued as an Oxford University Press paperback 1984

British Library Cataloguing in Publication Data

Bates, H. E.
My Uncle Silas.—(Twentieth century
classics).—(Oxford paperbacks)
I. Title   II. Series
823'.912[F] PR6003.A965
ISBN 0-19-281854-6

Library of Congress Cataloging in Publication Data

Bates, H. E. (Herbert Ernest), 1905-1974.
My Uncle Silas. (Twentieth century classics) (Oxford paperbacks)
Originally published: London: J. Cape, [1939]
I. Title.   II. Series.
PR6003.A965M9 1984   823'.912   84-9672
ISBN 0-19-281854-6 (pbk.)

Printed in Great Britain by
Richard Clay (The Chaucer Press) Ltd
Bungay, Suffolk

INTRODUCTION

BY V. S. PRITCHETT

THE short story is the most *memorable* form of fiction. It is memorable because it has to tell and ring in every line. It has to be as exact as a sonnet or a ballad. It is, in essence, 'poetic' in its impulse. We do not forget it, indeed find more and more in it, whereas even in the greatest novels we easily forget whole chapters. Also, the short story is very suited to the nervous, glancing habits forced upon us by the hurry of contemporary life, which is so unlike the ruminative life of the nineteenth century when the novel was the dominating form of fiction. In the novel we lose ourselves; in the shorter thing we find ourselves. At the end of the nineteenth century we meet the first outstanding masters of the form in Kipling, Wells, Conrad, James; in artists like Katherine Mansfield, Saki, Liam O'Flaherty, Frank O'Connor, D. H. Lawrence, the Joyce of *Dubliners* and many others. They have read Maupassant, Chekhov and Turgenev. Their special gift is to catch the crucial moments of a life as it passes. We see people who might have been minor characters in great novels, but now enlarged and brought forward.

H. E. Bates was one of the gifted English artists in the genre, especially in what he wrote in the Twenties and Thirties. He was a poet by nature. His setting was usually the traditional life of the small farms, cottages and holdings, his people the hedgers, ditchers, thatchers and local carriers—a horse-and-cart England

3

in the main, the England of rural hagglings and feelings which had changed very little for centuries and often sounds Chaucerian and ripe in speech. We know how his people talk, eat, work, drink, love and die. Their habits had not yet been touched by the industrialization which changed village life after the last war. The people are not the generalized 'Loamshire' folk of radio and television, and for that reason are real in their past. If Bates's temperament was poetic, he was not a prettifier of archaic things. Bates's people and landscape are marvellously seen afresh. In the mere account of a man and boy ploughing or a woman leaning on a gate in fitful spring weather we see not only the day as it passes but how the people, inarticulate as they may be, feel their lives passing. For his evocations of such weathering of men, women and country he has been compared to Hardy; but he is without Hardy's Darwinian melancholy, Hardy's large speculations about class or social tendencies, or his sententious and fateful regard for the pagan and indifferent 'President of the Immortals'. Bates is interested in people for their own curious sakes. In one of his finest stories, *The Mill*, a tragedy is left to tell itself. It is a tragedy set in motion by the meanness of a country trader in scrap. Bates was often lyrical but here he exposed the sourness and silences of rural poverty and the unprotected sight of innocence abused. The story has remained in my mind for forty years. But Bates was a writer of many kinds of stories. He could be lyrical, dour, even luscious and comic too. In the remarkable *The Woman who had Imagination* we shall see a vulgar group of cheery villagers boozing, itching and singing on a charabanc trip to give a rural concert in the grounds of a country house; and in the series

4

INTRODUCTION

of stories called *My Uncle Silas* hear a genial rapscallion in his nineties telling extravagant lies about his sinful life to a boy.

Do not mistake the Uncle Silas stories for old-style bucolic farce. Every detail of Silas's unwashed ugliness and of his domestic habits as the village liar and boozer is truthfully put before us, as if we were sitting in his house with him or had been sent down to the cellar to bring up another dreadful bottle of his home-made wine. And Bates has had the art to make us see the villain through the memory of a small boy who is fascinated by the old man, if also, every now and then, sceptical. Silas has the arts of the rural story-teller who drops into long evasive silences and then takes up the tale to add to its enormities, deedily watching his audience. Cats come out of the bag one at a time: that is art and artfulness. He can suggest even more by an unfinished phrase, by a mastery of innocent metaphor or *double entendre*. The boy will believe the old man is, for example, talking to a girl about duck eggs but the old man is insinuating some other attraction. He is a great guzzler, but having a boy before him he is free to boast that in his time there has been nothing he has not eaten—once, out of desperate necessity, iron nails. And not only iron nails, but nails made digestible by a paste of shavings from a rotten cellar floor. To prove it he opens his mouth and shows how the enforced diet has left rusty stains on his remaining teeth. But why *enforced*? A girl he was carrying on with shut him in the cellar when she saw her husband about to catch him. Which girl? Ah! Silence; but a glance to the scrawny, hot-tempered old housekeeper who has come in to make the old fellow strip naked so that she can give him

5

something he detests—his weekly bath in a tub by the fire—suggests all.

Is Uncle Silas a preposterous exaggeration? Not entirely, for two reasons. Bates knows how to make silences pregnant and then the boy is his passive, wondering audience. The listening of the boy makes the stories almost genuine. The second justification is that Uncle Silas is an expert in the techniques of rural story-telling, that is to say he is the villager talking, when an hour will pass while one person and then the next will join in and add some fantasy out of village memory to the tale. He is rumour itself. It will succeed if told in a flat, casually dry passage; until it reaches an open-ended silence for the next speaker to go one better, out of village memory. Uncle Silas is in fact the scandalizing village memory at work. One is listening to something in the genre of *The Miller's Tale*; and, in any case, every villager has samples of every kind of man and woman in the world at hand. Well, not every kind, but some very insinuating examples. Like most good short stories from Chekhov onwards, Bates had the art that enabled him to write many kinds of story. The poet could be the comedian, saved from slapstick by his resources of style and observation. And he was always at his best in the country landscape of his childhood where the hours seemed fuller and longer.

CONTENTS

PREFACE

IN the graveyard of one of the pleasantest villages in Bedfordshire, standing in the undulating beautifully wooded country that is typical of that part of the Ouse Valley, there lies buried a certain Joseph Betts, late husband of my maternal grandmother's sister Mary Ann, herself the most exquisite cook of a floury potato, with butter sauce, that ever lived in that district. This Joseph Betts, born at the very beginning of the Hungry 'Forties, brought up to a Church in which the serpent was still part of the Sunday morning orchestra, able to recall the arrival of news of the Crimea by a messenger from London on a white horse, was the original of my Uncle Silas.

I have always thought it a fatal policy for an author to set out to explain his own work, but there are points about my Uncle Silas, and his original, in which the reading public may be interested. It is not often that a short-story writer succeeds, even by accident, in producing a character which continues to develop an existence through several stories, unless that character happens to be himself. And when, five or six years ago, I wrote the first of these stories, *The Lily*, it did not for a moment occur to me to repeat or develop this picture of a rural reprobate. When I did repeat it, in *The Wedding* and *The Death of Uncle Silas*, I was astonished to find that a large public had already acclaimed it and was apparently ready to go on acclaiming it enthusiastically.

PREFACE

The Death of Uncle Silas produced, in fact, a larger volume of correspondence than any full-length book of mine has done before or since: a delighted but protesting correspondence, in which Americans and Colonials, English and Irish, critics and all kinds of unknown people, demanded the resurrection of Uncle Silas as soon as possible.

The ultimate result of that demand is this book. The English character still contains in it, generally, very strong elements of the Puritan. You see it at its fiercest, in conflict, in artists like D. H. Lawrence, at its pettiest in magistrates who remonstrate with young ladies who appear in court without stockings or reprove young men who appear in sports coats. But now and then the stream of the original Adam, rich and lusty and robust, comes straight through, undiluted and unpurified. This strong original devilishness spouts up in characters like my Uncle Silas, who, it is significant to note, spent his life of more than ninety years in a district which still flaunts its sprig of oak-leaves for King Charles on the 29th of May: an unconscious protest against the Puritanical poison in the English blood. Certainly there was no strain of the Puritan in my Uncle Silas, who got gloriously and regularly drunk, loved food and the ladies and good company, was not afraid to wear a huge and flamboyant buttonhole, told lies, got the better of his fellow-men whenever the chance offered itself, used a scythe like an angel, was a wonderful gardener, took the local lord's pheasants, and yet succeeded in remaining an honest, genuine and lovable character.

Silas is, therefore, an authentic figure. The scenes and

incidents in which he appears are, too, very close to life. The picture of his small thatched house, the sun-steeped garden with its flowers and gooseberry-trees, the Maiden's Blush rose flowering by the open door, the scarlet lily itself, the wood with its wild strawberries, the surrounding meadows rich with meadowsweet and pink orchis and moon-daisy, are all things which have the dearest associations for me in memory. Consequently certain stories, in particular *The Lily*, *The Wedding*, which my sister and I still remember as one of the golden days of our childhood, *The Revelation*, since Silas in plain truth never washed himself, *Silas the Good*, which is almost as he himself related it to me, and *The Death of Uncle Silas*, are all so near to reality that they needed only the slightest recolouring on my part. Others, notably *The Race*, *A Funny Thing*, and *A Happy Man*, have been inspired by that sort of apocryphal legend which is the inheritance of every country child who keeps his ears cocked when men are talking. To those who find these stories too Rabelaisian, far-fetched or robust, my reply would be that, as pictures of English country life, they are in reality understated.

Finally, since memory is inexhaustible, there seems to be no reason why, within proper limits, this happy lusty and devilish character, who was up to all the tricks for nearly a hundred years, should not have spirit enough to fill another story or two beyond these pages. If that should happen it is my great hope that I shall again be lucky enough to have the collaboration of Mr. Edward Ardizzone, whose crabbed and crusty pictures are so absolutely and perfectly in the spirit of every page they illustrate.   H. E. BATES

THE LILY

THE LILY

M Y Great-uncle Silas used to live in a small stone reed-thatched cottage on the edge of a pine-wood, where nightingales sang passionately in great numbers through early summer nights and on into the mornings and often still in the afternoons. On summer days after rain the air was sweetly saturated with the fragrance of the pines, which mingled subtly with the exquisite honeysuckle scent, the strange vanilla heaviness from the creamy elder-flowers in the garden hedge and the perfume of old pink and white crimped-double roses of forgotten names. It was very quiet there except for the soft, water-whispering sound of leaves and boughs, and the squabbling and singing of birds in the house-thatch and the trees. The house itself was soaked with years of scents, half-sweet, half-dimly-sour with the smell of wood smoke, the curious odour of mauve and milk-coloured and red geraniums, of old wine and tea and the earth smell of my Uncle Silas himself.

It was the sort of house to which old men retire to enjoy their last days. Shuffling about in green carpet-slippers, they do nothing but poke the fire, gloomily clip their beards, read the newspapers with their spectacles on upside down, take too much physic and die of boredom at last.

But my Uncle Silas was different. At the age of ninety-three he was as lively and restless as a young colt. He shaved every morning at half-past five with cold water and a razor

older than himself which resembled an antique barbaric bill-hook. He still kept alive within him some gay, devilish spark of audacity which made him attractive to the ladies. He ate too much and he drank too much.

'God strike me if I tell a lie,' he used to say, 'but I've drunk enough beer, me boyo, to float the fleet and a drop over.'

I remember seeing him on a scorching, windless day in July. He ought to have been asleep in the shade with his red handkerchief over his old walnut-coloured face, but when I arrived he was at work on his potato-patch, digging steadily and strongly in the full blaze of the sun.

Hearing the click of the gate he looked up, and seeing me, waved his spade. The potato-patch was at the far end of the long garden, where the earth was warmest under the wood-side, and I walked down the long path to it between rows of fat-podded peas and beans and full-fruited bushes of currant and gooseberry. By the house, under the sun-white wall, the sweet-williams and white pinks flamed softly against the hot marigolds and the orange poppies flat opened to drink in the sun.

'Hot,' I said.

'Warmish.' He did not pause in his strong, rhythmical digging. The potato-patch had been cleared of its crop and the sun-withered haulms had been heaped against the hedge.

'Peas?' I said. The conversation was inevitably laconic.

'Taters,' he said. He did not speak again until he had dug to the edge of the wood. There he straightened his back, blew his nose on his red handkerchief, let out a nonchalant flash of spittle, and cocked his eye at me.

'Two crops,' he said. 'Two crops from one bit o' land. How's that, me boyo? Every heard talk o' that?'

'Never.'

'And you'd be telling a lie if you said you had. Because I know you ain't.'

He winked at me, with that swift cock of the head and the perky flicker of the lid that had in it all the saucy jauntiness of a youth of twenty. He was very proud of himself. He was doing something extraordinary and he knew it. There was no humbug about him.

Sitting in the low shade of the garden hedge I watched him, waiting for him to finish digging. He was a short, thick-built man, and his old corduroy trousers concertina-folded over his squat legs and his old wine-red waistcoat ruckled up over his heavy chest made him look dwarfer and thicker still. He was as ugly as some old Indian idol, his skin walnut-stained and scarred like a weather-cracked apple, his cheeks hanging loose and withered, his lips wet and almost sensual and a trifle sardonic with their sideways twist and the thick pout of the lower lip. His left eye was bloodshot, a thin vein or two of scarlet staining the white, but he kept the lid half-shut, only raising it abruptly now and then with an odd cocking-flicker that made him look devilish and sinister. The sudden gay, jaunty flash of his eyes was electric, immortal. I told him once that he'd live to be a thousand. 'I shall,' he said.

When he had finished the digging and was scraping the light sun-dry soil from his spade with his flattened thumb I got up languidly from under the hedge.

'Don't strain yourself,' he said.

He shouldered his spade airily and walked away towards the house and I followed him, marvelling at his age, his strength, and his tirelessness under that hot sun. Half-way up the garden path he stopped to show me his gooseberries. They were as large as young green peaches. He gathered a handful, and the bough, relieved of the weight, swayed up swiftly from the earth. When I had taken a gooseberry he threw the rest into his mouth, crunching them like a horse eating fresh carrots. Something made me say, as I sucked the gooseberry:

'You must have been born about the same year as Hardy.'

'Hardy?' He cocked his bloodshot eye at me. 'What Hardy?'

'Thomas Hardy.'

He thought a moment, crunching gooseberries.

'I recollect him. Snotty little bit of a chap, red hair, always had a dew-drop on the end of his nose. One o' them Knotting Fox Hardies. Skinny lot. I recollect him.'

'No, not him. I mean another Hardy. Different man.'

'Then he was afore my time.'

'No, he was about your time. You must have heard of him. He wrote books.'

The word finished him: he turned and began to stride off towards the house. 'Books,' I heard him mutter, 'Books!' And suddenly he turned on me and curled his wet red lips and said in a voice of devastating scorn, his bloodshot eye half-angry, half-gleeful:

'I daresay.' And then in a flash: 'But could he grow goosegogs like that?"

Without pausing for an answer, he strode off again, and I followed him up the path and out of the blazing white afternoon sun into the cool, geranium-smelling house, and there he sat down in his shirt-sleeves in the big black-leathered chair that he once told me his grandmother had left him, with a hundred pounds sewn in the seat that he sat on for ten years without knowing it.

'Mouthful o' wine?' he said to me softly, and then before I had time to answer he bawled into the silence of the house:

'Woman! If you're down the cellar bring us a bottle o' cowslip!'

'I'm upstairs,' came a voice.

'Then come down. And look slippy.'

'Fetch it yourself!'

'What's that, y'old tit? I'll fetch you something you won't forget in a month o' Sundays. D'ye hear?' There was a low muttering and rumbling over the ceiling. 'Fetch it yourself,' he muttered. 'Did ye hear that? Fetch it yourself!'

'I'll fetch it,' I said.

'You sit down,' he said. 'What do I pay a housekeeper for? Sit down. She'll bring it.'

I sat down in the broken-backed chair that in summer time always stood by the door, propping it open. The deep roof dropped a strong black shadow across the threshold but outside the sun blazed unbrokenly, with a still, intense midsummer light. There was no sound or movement from anything except the bees, droll and drunken, as they crawled and tippled down the yellow and blue and dazzling white throats of the flowers. And sitting there waiting for the wine to come up, listening to the bees working down into the heart of the silence, I saw a flash of scarlet in the garden, and said:

'I see the lily's in bloom.'

And as though I had startled him, Uncle Silas looked up quickly, almost with suspicion.

'Ah, she's in bloom,' he said.

I was wondering why he always spoke of the lily as though it were a woman, when the housekeeper, her unlaced shoes clip-clopping defiantly on the wooden cellar-steps and the brick passage, came in with a green wine-bottle, and, slapping it down on the table, went out again with her head stiffly uplifted, without a word.

'Glasses!' yelled my Uncle Silas.

'Bringing 'em if you can wait!' she shouted back.

'Well, hurry then! And don't fall over yourself!'

She came back a moment or two later with the glasses, which she clapped down on the table just as she had done the wine-bottle, defiantly, without a word. She was a scraggy, frosty-eyed woman, with a tight, almost lipless mouth, and as she stalked out of the door my Uncle Silas leaned across to me and said in a whisper just loud enough for her to hear:

'Tart as a stick of old rhubarb.'

'What's that you're saying?' she said at once.

'Never spoke. Never opened me mouth.'

'I heard you!'

'Go and put yourself in curling pins, you old straight hook!'

'I'm leaving,' she shouted.

'Leave!' he shouted. 'And good riddance.'

'Who're you talking to, eh? Who're you talking to, you corrupted old devil? You ought to be ashamed of yourself! If you weren't so old I'd warm your breeches till you couldn't sit down. I'm off.'

She flashed out, clip-clopping with her untied shoes along the passage and upstairs while he chanted after her, in his devilish, goading voice:

'Tart as a bit of old rhubarb! Tart as a bit of old rhubarb!'

When the house was silent again he looked at me and winked his bloodshot eye and said 'Pour out,' and I filled the tumblers with the clear sun-coloured wine. As we drank I said, 'You've done it now,' and he winked back at me again, knowing that I knew that she had been leaving every day for twenty years, and that they had quarrelled with each other day and night for nearly all that time, secretly loving it.

Sitting by the door, sipping the sweet, cold wine, I looked at the lily again. Its strange, scarlet, turk's-cap blossoms had just begun to uncurl in the July heat, the colour hot and passionate against the snow-coloured pinks and the cool larkspurs and the stiff spikes of the madonnas, sweet and virgin, but like white wax. Rare, exotic, strangely lovely, the red lily had blossomed there, untouched, for as long as I could remember.

'When are you going to give me a little bulb off the lily?' I said.

'You know what I've always told you,' he said. 'You can have her when I'm dead. You can come and dig her up then. Do what you like with her.'

I nodded. He drank, and as I watched his skinny throat filling and relaxing with the wine I said:

'Where did you get it? In the first place?'

He looked at the almost empty glass.

'I pinched her,' he said.

'How?'

'Never mind. Give us another mouthful o' wine.'

He held out his glass, and I rose and took the wine-bottle from the table and paused with my hand on the cork. 'Go on,' I said, 'tell me.'

'I forget,' he said. 'It's been so damn long ago.'

'How long?'

'I forget,' he said.

As I gave him back his wine-filled glass I looked at him with a smile and he smiled back at me, half-cunning, half-sheepish, as though he knew what I was thinking. He possessed the vividest memory, a memory he often boasted about as he told me the stories of his boyhood, rare tales of prize-fights on summer mornings by isolated woods very long ago, of how he heard the news of the Crimea, of how he took a candle to church to warm his hands against it in the dead of winter, and how when the parson cried out 'And he shall see a great light, even as I see one now!' he snatched up the candle in fear of hell and devils and sat on it. 'And I can put my finger on the spot now.'

By that smile on his face I knew that he remembered about the lily, and after taking another long drink of the wine he began to talk. His voice was crabbed and rusty, a strong, ugly voice that had no softness or tenderness in it, and his half-shut, bloodshot eye and his wet, curled lips looked rakish and wicked, as though he were acting the villainous miser in one of those travelling melodramas of his youth.

'I seed her over in a garden, behind a wall,' he said. 'Big wall, about fifteen feet high. We were banging in hard a-carrying hay and I was on the top o' the cart and could see her just over the wall. Not just one—scores, common as poppies. I felt I shouldn't have no peace again until I had one. And I nipped over the wall that night about twelve o'clock and ran straight into her.'

'Into the lily?'

'Tah! Into a gal. See? Young gal—about my age, daughter o' the house. All dressed in thin white. "What are you doing here?" she says, and I believe she was as frit as I was. "I lost something," I says. "It's all right. You know me." And then she wanted to know what I'd lost, and I felt as if I didn't care what happened, and I said, "Lost my head, I reckon." And she laughed, and then I laughed and then she said, "Ssshhh! Don't you see I'm as done as you are if we're found here? You'd better go. What did you come for, anyway?" And I told her. She wouldn't believe me. "It's right," I says, "I just come for the lily." And she just stared at me. "And you

23

know what they do to people who steal?" she says. "Yes," I says, and they were the days when you could be hung for looking at a sheep almost. "But picking flowers ain't stealing," I says. "Ssshhh!" she says again. "What d'ye think I'm going to say if they find me here? Don't talk so loud. Come here behind these trees and keep quiet." And we went and sat down behind some old box-trees and she kept whispering about the lily and telling me to whisper for fear anyone should come. "I'll get you the lily all right," she says, "if you keep quiet. I'll dig it up." '

He ceased talking, and after the sound of his harsh, uncouth racy voice the summer afternoon seemed quieter than ever, the drowsy, stumbling boom of the bees in the July flowers only deepening the hot drowsy silence. I took a drink of the strong, cool, flower-odoured wine and waited for my Uncle Silas to go on with the story, but nothing happened, and finally I looked up at him.

'Well?' I said. 'What happened?'

For a moment or two he did not speak. But finally he turned and looked at me with a half-solemn, half-vivacious expression, one eye half-closed, and told me in a voice at once dreamy, devilish, innocent, mysterious and triumphant, all and more than I had asked to know.

'She gave me the lily,' he said.

THE REVELATION

THE REVELATION

MY Great-uncle Silas was a man who never washed himself. 'God A'mighty,' he would say, 'why should I? It's a waste o' time. I got summat else to do 'sides titivate myself wi' soap.' For years his housekeeper washed him instead.

Every morning, winter and summer, he sat in the high-backed chair under the window of geraniums waiting for that inexorable performance. He would sit there in a pretence of being engrossed in the newpaper of the day before, his waistcoat on but undone over his collarless blue shirt, his red neckerchief dangling on the arm of the chair, his face gloomy and long with the wretchedness of expectation. Sometimes he would lower the corner of the newspaper and squint out in the swift but faint hope that she had forgotten him. She never did. She would come out at last with the bowl of water and the rank cake of yellow soap that he would say she had been suckled on, and the rough hand-flannel that she had made up from some staunch undergarment she had at last discarded. In winter the water, drawn straight from the well, would be as bitter and stinging as ice. She never heated it. And as though her own hands had lost all feeling she would plunge them straight into it, and then rub the soap against the flannel until it lathered thinly, like snow. All the time he sat hidden behind the newspaper with a kind of dumb hope, like an ostrich. At last, before he knew what was

happening, the paper would be snatched from his hands, the flannel, like a cold compress, would be smacked against his face, and a shudder of utter misery would pass through his body before he began to pour forth the first of his blasphemous protestations. 'God damn it, woman! You want to finish me, don't you? You want to finish me! You want me to catch me death, you old nanny-goat! I know. You want me . . .' The words and their effect would be drowned and smothered by the renewed sopping of the flannel and he would be forced at last into a miserable acquiescence. It was the only time when the look of devilish vitality and wickedness left his face and never seemed likely to return.

Once a week, also, she succeeded in making him take a bath. She gave him that, too.

The house was very old and its facilities for bathing and washing were such that it might have been built expressly for him. There was no bathroom. My Uncle Silas had instead a small iron bath, once painted cream and never repainted after the cream had turned to the colour of earth, which resembled some ancient coracle. And once a week, generally on Fridays and always in the evening, the housekeeper would drag out the bath from among the wine-bottles in the cellar and bring it up and get it before the fire in the living-room. Once, in early summer, as though hoping it might make that miserable inquisition of bathing impossible, he had filled the bath with a pillow-case of cowslip heads and their own wine-yellow liquor. It did not deter her. She gave him his bath in a pudding-basin instead, sponging him down with water that grew cooler and colder as he stood there blaspheming and shivering.

Very often on fine winter evenings I would walk over to see him, and once, almost forgetting that it was his bath-night, I went over on a Friday.

When I arrived the house was oppressively warm with the heat and steam from the copper boiling up the bath-water in the little kitchen. I went in, as I always did, without knocking, and I came straight upon my Uncle Silas taking off his trousers, unconcerned, before a great fire of hazel faggots in the living-room.

'Oh! It's you,' he said. 'I thought for a minute it might be a young woman.'

'You ought to lock the door,' I said.

'God A'mighty, I ain't frit at being looked at in me bath. He held his trousers momentarily suspended, as though in deference to me. 'Never mattered to me since that day when . . .'

He broke off suddenly as the housekeeper came running in with the first bucket of boiling water for the bath, elbowing us out of her way, the water falling into the bath like a scalding waterfall. No sooner had the great cloud of steam dispersed than she was back again with a second bucket. It seemed hotter than the first.

'Out of my way!' she ordered.

'Git us a glass o' wine,' said Silas, 'and don't vapour about so much.'

'You'll have no wine,' she said, 'until you've been in that bath.'

31

'Then git us a dozen taters to roast. And look slippy.' She was already out of the door with the empty bucket. 'Get 'em yourself!' she flashed.

'I got me trousers off!' he shouted.

'Then put 'em on again!'

This relentless exchange of words went on all the time she was bringing the remaining buckets of water in and he was undoing the tapes of his pants, he shouting for the wine and the potatoes and she never wavering in her tart refusals to get them. Finally as he began to roll down his pants and she began to bring in the last buckets of water he turned to me and said:

'Git a light and go down and fetch that bottle o' wine and the taters. Bring a bottle of elderberry. A quart.'

While I was down in the cellar, searching with a candle in the musty, wine-odoured corners for the potatoes and the bottle, I could hear the faint sounds of argument and splashing water from above. I was perhaps five minutes in the cellar, and when I went back up the stone steps, with the wine in one hand and the candle in the other and the potatoes in my pockets, the sound of voices seemed to have increased.

When I reached the living-room Silas was standing up in the bath, stark naked, and the housekeeper was shouting:

'Sit down, man, can't you? Sit down! How can I bath you if you don't sit down?'

'Sit down yourself! I don't want to burn the skin off me behind, if you do!'

While he protested she seized his shoulders and tried to

force him down in the bath, but his old and rugged body, looking even stronger and more imperishable in its nakedness than ever, was stiff and immovable, and he never budged except to dance a little as the water stung the tender parts of his feet.

'Git the taters under!' he said to me at last. 'God A'mighty, I'll want summat after this.'

Gradually, as I was putting the potatoes in the ashes under the fire, the arguments quietened a little, and finally my Uncle Silas stooped, half-knelt in the water and then with a brief mutter of relief sat down. Almost in silence, the house-keeper lathered the flannel she had made from her petticoat and then proceeded to wash his body, scrubbing every inch of it fiercely, taking no more notice of his nakedness than if he had been a figure of wood. All the time he sat there a little abjectly, his spirit momentarily subdued, making no effort to wash himself except sometimes to dabble his hands and dribble a little water over his bony legs. He gave even that up at last, turning to me to say:

'I never could see a damn lot o' use in water.'

Finally when she had washed him all over, she seized the great coarse towel that had been warming on the clothes-horse by the fire.

'You're coming out now,' she said.

'I don't know as I am.'

'Did you hear what I said? You're coming out!'

'Damn, you were fast enough gittin' me in—you can wait a minute. I just got settled.'

Seizing his shoulders, she began to try to force him to

stand up just as she had tried to force him, only a minute or two before, to sit down. And as before he would not budge. He sat there luxuriously, not caring, some of the old devilish look of perversity back in his face, his hands playing with the water.

'He's just doing it on purpose,' she said to me at last. 'Just because you're here. He wants us to sit here and admire him. That's all. I know.'

'Don't talk so much!' he said. 'I'm getting out as fast as you'll let me.'

'Come on, then. Come on!' she insisted. 'Heaven knows we don't want to look at you all night.'

The words seemed to remind my Uncle Silas of something, and as he stood up in the bath and she began towelling his back, he said to me:

'I recollect what I was going to tell you now. I was having a swim with a lot o' chaps, once, in the mill-brook at . . .'

'We don't want to hear your old tales, either?' she said. 'We heard 'em all times anew.'

'Not this one,' he said.

Nevertheless, her words silenced him. He stood there dumb and almost meek all the time she was towelling him dry and it was only when she vanished into the kitchen to fetch a second towel for him to dry his toes that he recollected the story he had been trying to tell me, and came to life.

'I was swimming with these chaps, in the mill-brook, and we left all our clothes on the bank . . .'

'Mind yourselves!'

The housekeeper had returned with the towel, and my Uncle Silas, as though he had never even heard of the tale he was so anxious to tell and I was so anxious to hear, said solemnly to me:

'Next year I'll have peas where I had taters, and taters where I had carrots . . .'

'Dry your toes!' said the housekeeper.

'Dry 'em yourself and don't talk so much!'

At the same moment she thrust the towel in his hand and then began to scoop the water out of the bath with an enamel basin and put in into a bucket. When the bucket was full she hastened out of the room with it, her half-laced shoes slopping noisily in her haste. Almost before she had gone through the door and long before we heard the splash of water in the sink my Uncle Silas said swiftly 'Tot out,' and I uncorked the wine-bottle while he found the glasses in the little cupboard above the fire.

We were standing there drinking the wine, so red and rich and soft, Silas in nothing but his shirt, when the housekeeper returned. She refilled the bucket quickly and hastened out again. No sooner had she gone than he turned to me to continue the story, and standing there, his thick, blue-striped flannel shirt reaching below his knees, the hairs on his thin, gnarled legs standing out as stiff as the bristles on his own gooseberries, the wine-glass in one hand and the towel in the other, he looked more wicked and devilish and ugly than I ever remembered seeing him.

Going on with the story, he had reached the point when

the men, coming out of the mill-stream, had found their clothes gone, when the housekeeper returned.

'I think I s'll have peas along the side o' the wood,' he said, serenely while she refilled the bucket, 'and perhaps back o' the well.'

'You get your toes dried and get dressed!' she ordered.

'And you mind your own business and get the supper. And look slippy!'

As soon as she had left the room again, he resumed the tale, but no sooner had he begun than she returned. It went on like this, he telling a sentence of the tale, and she returning and he interspersing some angelic and airy remark about his peas and potatoes until at last she came in to spread the cloth on the table and lay the supper. She was in the room for so long, laying out the plates and the cutlery, that at last he gave it up, turning to me with an air of satanic innocence to say:

'I'll tell you the name 'o the tater when I can think of it. My memory ain't so good as it was.'

After that he proceeded meekly to put on his pants, tucking in the voluminous folds of his shirt before tying up the tapes. While the tail of his shirt was still hanging loose he remembered the potatoes I had put in the hot ashes under the fire and, seizing the toasting-fork, he began to prod their skins.

'Damn, they'll be done afore I get my trousers on,' he said. And standing there, with the toasting-fork in his hand, his pants tight against his legs and the tail of his shirt protruding he looked more than anything else like the devil of tradition, prodding the roasting sinners.

The veritable air of devilishness was still about him when, finding a moment later that the housekeeper had left the room again, he turned swiftly to me to say:

'Give us another mouthful o' wine. I'll tell you what happened.'

I had hardly begun to pour the wine into his glass before he began to say, in a devilish, husky voice that was hardly more than a whisper: 'Some gals had got the clothes. They stood upon the bridge and dangled our trousers over and threatened to drop 'em in the mill-pond. What d'ye think of that? There we were swimming about wi' nothing on and they wouldn't give us the clothes.'

He went on to tell me how gradually they grew tired and desperate and at last angry at the three girls dangling over the bridge while they grew colder and colder in the deep mill-pool and how finally he himself climbed out of the water and ran up to the bridge, stark naked, and frightened the girls into dropping the clothes and retreating. Long before he had finished I noticed that the housekeeper had returned and was standing in the doorway, unseen by my Uncle Silas, attentively listening.

'God A'mighty, you should have seen 'em drop the clothes and run when they see me. All except one.'

'What did she do?'

'Run off across the meadow with my clothes under her arms. What d'ye think o' that?'

'What did you do?'

'Run after her.'

He ceased speaking, and taking a slow drink of his wine

he moistened his thick, red lips with his tongue, as though the tale were not finished and he were trying to remember its end. A strange almost soft expression of reminiscence came over his face, flushed with the bath and the wine, as though he could see clearly the river, the meadow, and he himself running across the summer grass, naked, pursuing the girl running away with his clothes.

'Rum un,' he said at last. 'I never did find out who she was. Never did find out.'

At that moment the housekeeper came in from the door-way, moving so quietly for once that he scarcely heard her, the sound of the cheese-dish being laid on the table startling him so much that he could only turn and stare at her, fingering the tapes of his pants and at a loss for words.

'Didn't you ever find out?' she said.

'No. I was just telling the boy. It's been so damn long ago.'

She looked at him for a moment and then said:

'I know who she was. And so do you.'

It was the only time I ever saw him at a loss for an answer and it was almost the only time I ever saw her smile. He stood there slowly licking his lips in uneasy silence until at last she snapped at him with all the old habitual tartness:

'Get yourself dressed, man! I ain't running away with your clothes now, if I did then.'

She began to help him on with his clothes. He still had nothing to say, but once, as she was fastening the back buttons of his trousers and he stood with his face turned away from her, he gave me a smiling but inscrutable look,

rich with devilry, his eyelids lowered and his lips shining wet with the wine.

And I began to understand then something I had not understood before.

THE WEDDING

THE WEDDING

I WAS seven or eight and my Great-uncle Silas nearly seventy when his only son Abel was married to a girl named Georgina, and we all drove over for the wedding in the black-and-yellow trap with the white racy-looking horse, my grandparents and parents, my aunt and I, before the dew had dried on the buttercupped grass one May morning. The air was rich and summery and the sun was a long time breaking through the mist as we drove along. The wedding had come upon us suddenly. The girl, Georgina, had arrived that springtime to be a lady's maid at the house where Abel had been a gardener for nearly twenty years. It was all over in a month; done, as my grandfather said, all of a damn pop. Nor did my grandmother like it; she was a little, pale woman, like a faded canary and as quick-tongued, and as she sat perched up on the high trap seat in her grey and purple silk I thought she looked as if she would like to peck at the creature who had seduced a solid, hard-hatted fellow like Abel with such indecent haste. Abel was nearly forty and the girl, it seemed, was only nineteen. But it was to be a great wedding.

We talked of it as we drove along. 'I should think,' said my grandmother, 'he's well set to work, marrying a filly like that. Nineteen!' But my grandfather had seen the girl.

'Dall it all,' he kept saying, 'she's flash. And don't she

42

talk nice! Jest so. Ho dear, ho dear! I tell you she's lovely.'

'Yes, and without a farden to bless herself with, I'll be bound. Who's paying for the flash wedding?'

'Silas, I expect.'

'Ah,' said my grandmother, 'and I'd Silas him if I were Sarah Ann. I remember the last wedding we went to with Silas.'

My grandfather evidently remembered it too. He suddenly looked embarrassed, nudged my arm, and pointed with his driving whip at a cuckoo flying fast across a field of beans, calling as it flew, its voice trembling with the motion of its flight. My grandfather followed the bird until it alighted, far off, in an ash tree, and then he nudged me again and told me to look up, straight above, at a lark breaking into passionate song, and we turned our faces to the sun-misty sky and watched the bird twittering up and up, out of sight.

'You'll get something you don't expect,' my grandmother warned us, 'cocking your eyes at that bird.'

'Tchk! Tchk!' said my grandfather to the horse.

'And *look* at you!' exclaimed my grandmother, suddenly. 'Whoa! I never saw such a man in all my born days. You'll be hanging yourself in the reins next.'

'Whoa!' said my grandfather gloomily.

The horse stopped and my grandmother leaned across me and seized my grandfather's collar, which had sprung away from its stud, catapulting his necktie away and releasing his white starched dicky from its top buttonhole.

'Hold still,' urged my grandmother. 'That comes of gaping at birds instead of driving on as you should do.' She fixed the collar, smoothed the tie and flattened the dicky, and my grandfather, looking extremely meek and ill at ease in the iron-starched collar and front and his best black clothes and hard hat, drove on again, straining his sun-tanned neck so that the guides tautened in agony. 'Lord, man, anybody'd think you'd been hung,' said my grandmother.

As we drove on the mist began to disperse, the sun shining through at first softly and at last with the strong thundery heat of the May morning. 'I don't know,' said my grandmother, as though in hope, 'as that girl ain't going to have a wet ride after all.'

It was five miles to my Uncle Silas's house, and though the wedding wasn't until two o'clock, we had started the journey at ten o'clock in the morning. There was no sense, declared my grandmother, in not making a day of it; nor, said my grandfather, did we want to wrench the guts out of the horse. So we had started early, and we drove along all the time at the same solemn pace, the horse never breaking into a trot, my grandfather never using the whip except to flick away the flies; and now and then we would stop, perhaps to admire a field of young barley, or to have a word by the roadside with a man my grandfather hadn't seen for a year, or to gaze at the bluebells staining the dark earth of the woods we passed. At every hill we stopped so that my parents and my grandmother and aunt could alight and walk up the hill. My grandfather and I remained in the trap, sitting well forward in the seat in order to relieve the strain on the horse. And once, going up a hill by a spinney, we heard a nightingale, and then another and another, singing fitfully, but with breaks of wild passion, in the young hazel trees. Cuckoos were calling continually in their full bold mocking, and when we stopped to listen it sounded as though the cuckoos were contradicting the nightingales, their monotonous cries half-drowning the others' wild spasmodic singing.

'We must ask your Uncle Silas,' said my grandfather, 'if he knows to a nightingale's.'

'He'll have enough to think on,' said my grandmother, 'with that other nightingale.'

It was nearly twelve o'clock when we arrived at my Uncle Silas's house, the little reed-thatched house standing at the top of the violet-banked lane by the spinney of pines. The lane, steep and narrow, was cobbled with white hoof-smooth stones, and at the bottom of it were all alighted, my grandfather and I leading the horse.

'Dall it,' exclaimed my grandfather as we came within sight of the house, 'can I see straight?'

We all stopped on the crest of the slope, and my grandmother let out an exclamation of tart astonishment:

'A tent! What the 'nation do they want with a tent? Ain't that just like Silas?'

'It might be Georgina's doing,' said my aunt. 'I heard she'd got money.'

'I'd Georgina her!' cried my grandmother as we went on. As we came nearer the house the tent which had been erected in Uncle Silas's paddock seemed larger than ever, a big square marquee like a sort of squat steeple, the canvas as white as the moon-daisies growing thicker than the grass in the field. Little yellow and green and blue and scarlet pennants fluttered above it listlessly, and its ropes were as clean as new straw. Long trestle tables had been erected both inside it and on the surrounding grass, and waiters in shirt-sleeves were already rushing hither and thither, spreading cloths even whiter than the tent, arranging flower-vases, carrying glasses and cups and plates and cutlery, salt-silvered hams and joints of beef and roast fowls and loaves and cheese, dark bottles of wine and cases of beer and stone-jars of home-made, unloading them from a wagon which had been drawn up before us by two satiny black horses with their ears in little silk nets and their tails plaited and tied with bows of white and cornflower-blue.

'It's a licker,' said my grandfather, who seemed, I thought, to be not so much astonished as delighted. 'Look at them bottles!'

'You look at what you're doing,' said my grandmother.

And very slowly we all walked on to the house, marvelling at the tent and the food-laden tables and the sweating waiters.

Just as we drew up behind the wagon an extraordinary figure in yellow corduroy trousers, a blue shirt, a red waist-coat and a squashed brown panama, came rushing excitedly out of the house carrying a tray of glasses and bottles with one hand and trying to keep up his trousers with the other. He was waddling on his thick bowed legs across the paddock, chuckling wickedly, when my grandmother arrested him.

'Silas!' she shouted. 'Do you want to blind us all?'

'Lord A'mighty,' said my Uncle Silas, 'I never seed you.'

He stopped abruptly and, still holding up his trousers, came rolling back across the paddock towards us.

I whispered to my mother, 'Why can't he walk straight?'

'Sshh!' she said. 'It's the heavy bottles.'

From the way in which my grandmother began to address my Uncles Silas it seemed as if it were the heavy bottles.

'Silas,' she said, 'you ought to be ashamed of yourself at twelve o'clock in the morning.'

'I am,' he said wickedly.

'And what's happened to your trousers?'

'They'll be down any minute.'

'Silas, you're not responsible! Where's Sarah Ann?'

'Gone down to church to titivate the altar.'

"I'll titivate you in a minute!' she threatened, and before Silas could move or speak she was off towards the house, nipping along in her inexorable, quick, bird-like fashion.

When she returned a moment or two later my Uncle Silas was already totting out for the waiters and my grandfather and himself, the beer in the glasses shining a rich tawny dandelion-gold in the noon sunlight. He was standing at one end of the long trestle-tables, pouring out beer with one hand and still holding up his trousers with the other, when she arrived behind him. He had no chance with her. 'Stand still,' she said, seizing his trousers. 'It's a darning needle,' and with her lips set tartly she proceeded to sew on his lost buttons, her hands spider-quick and neat with the thread. 'I'm surprised at you, Silas,' she would say. 'And if you touch that glass I'll prick you.'

My Uncle Silas stood with a sort of meek wickedness, winking at the waiters.

'And what about this girl?' said my grandmother. 'Didn't waste no time, did she?'

'Nor did you.'

'I said what about her?'

'Lovely.'

'And who's paying for all this—this tent an' all?'

'A markwee,' my Uncle Silas corrected her. 'A markwee.'

'Well, whatever it is. You ain't paying for it, I hope?'

'Lord Henry and Lady Hester,' said my Uncle Silas, 'are paying for every mite and mossel.'

'Everything?'

'Every drop and crumb.'

'And the tent?'

'And the markwee.'

My grandmother had no more to say. She was finished. She put the final stitch into my Uncle Silas's trousers and stuck the needle into some invisible place among her skirts. My Uncle Silas drank his beer at one draught, and my grandmother seemed to be so flabbergasted that she did not see him pour out another, not only for himself, but for my grandfather too.

She stalked off into the house, and my parents and my aunt followed her. My grandfather and I stayed with Uncle Silas and the waiters, marvelling at the meat and drink that the men kept unloading from the wagons. The heavy summer air, fragrant already with the scents of grass and roses and the old lilac trees near the garden, was thick also with the smell of meat and beer and new warm bread.

'I never seed hams like 'em,' marvelled my grandfather.

'No, and you never will again,' said my Uncle Silas.

We went into the marquee and marvelled again at the joints, the roast ducks and chickens, the salads and wines, the bright sherried trifles, the wine jellies, the strange sauces and cakes and finicking tit-bits and sweets all arranged on the long, white tables.

'Is there any mortal thing in the eatin' line as you ain't got, Silas?' said my grandfather.

'Nothing,' said my Uncle Silas.

'And where's Abel?'

'Skulking upstairs like a young leveret. Frit to death.'

When we left the marquee and went across the paddock towards the house my Uncle Silas bawled out:

'Abel!'

An upstairs window opened and Abel put his head out. Abel looked as though he had been carved crudely out of raw beef; he had a thick black wig of hair and the eyes of a mournful cow. There was something sleepy, simple, and pathetic about him. I believe my Uncle Silas was eternally ashamed of him.

'Damn it, man,' said my Uncle Silas, sharply, 'there's half the guests here a'ready and you still a-bed!'

'I ain't a-bed,' said Abel. 'I'm buttoning me shoes up.'

It was more than my Uncle Silas could stand. 'Buttoning me shoes up,' he muttered, waddling off. 'Buttoning me belly button.'

And following him, we went into the garden. There we heard the nightingales again, one against another, tuning up, half sharp, half sweet, their notes enriched by the sultry summer air under the shelter of the pines. The scent of lilac in the full heaviness of its blossoming was like a drug, marvellously fragrant. The green peas were bursting into white flower and the first roses were crimsoning the house wall, their glossy leaves splashed with the white droppings of the swallows flying to and fro to nest under the thatch-eaves.

All the time we were in the garden my Uncle Silas talked more garrulously and more excitedly than usual, and he was still very garrulous and excited when the cabs and wedding-flies drove up the lane to take us to church. And I remember saying to my mother again as he walked down the lane with us: 'Why can't he walk straight?'

'Ssh!' she whispered. 'It's this rough lane.'

We all drove to the church in flies and cabs drawn by white horses with polished hoofs and silk-ribboned bridles. There were more than a hundred guests, a great dazzle of white dresses and white buttonholes, and my Uncle Silas looked magnificent. There was a sort of purposely devilish splendour about his light grey coat and trousers, his yellow carnation, his canary waistcoat, and his grey square bowler rakishly cocked askew as though to match that everlastingly devilish look in his bloodshot eye.

'Well,' said my grandmother, 'it might be a skittle-match to look at Silas.'

The church was full, and I remember my grandfather

saying to me: 'Don't want to hear a lot o' popery and hymn-singing, do you?' and we stayed outside together, looking for nests in the churchyard yews and reading the names on the tombstones until the wedding was over.

It was not until then, when the church door opened and the guests and the congregation began to flock into the churchyard that I saw Georgina.

'Ain't she flash?' whispered my grandfather. 'Didn't I say so?'

She was unforgettably lovely. As she came from the church-porch with Abel, who looked more than ever solemn and simple in his suit of blue serge, his bowler hat, and his light brown button-boots which squeaked a little, she seemed to me more beautiful, more spirited, and more enchanting than perhaps she really was. She was very dark, her black hair and eyes shining vividly against her white wedding dress. Her face seemed full of a half-angelic, half-wicked vivacity and the conflicting lights and expressions of pure naivety and passion. She was across the churchyard and in the wedding-fly in a moment, and I did not see her again until we were all sitting about the long tables in the marquee eating and drinking and talking and laughing, with the sweating waiters rushing hither and thither, juggling with food and drink, madly trying to serve everyone at once.

And at the table-head, next to Georgina and Abel, sat my Uncle Silas, and opposite him Lord Henry and Lady Hester, for whom Georgina and Abel worked. Lord Henry put on an eyeglass and read a speech, 'Ee heev greet pleesyah,' and so on, which we all applauded by banging the tables, making the glass and crockery dance and ring. After him, I remember my Uncle Silas rose with a sort of noble unsteadiness to his feet, waved his hands, almost pitched forward, clutched the table in time, took a drink to steady himself, and began a long, tipsy speech, which we almost drowned with our table-banging and laughter, and of which all I can remember is a kind of refrain that he kept repeating as he gazed with a sort of sleepily wicked admiration at Georgina:

'Afore the night's gone we'll sing you a song. Me and the bride, eh?'

Georgina would smile without opening her lips, a mar-vellous, lovely, insinuating smile, and my Uncle Silas would wink and proceed with his speech, breaking now and then into long words which he could not pronounce with his drink-fuddled lips.

'Silas has swallowed the dictionary,' someone remarked.

'Don't know what it is,' declared Silas, lifting his glass, 'but it wants a hell of a lot o' washing down.'

I could see my grandmother fuming, her lips set thin with exasperation. 'You won't catch me at another wedding with Silas,' she said, 'as long as I live. Not if I know it.'

'Silas,' she said to him, severely, when the feast was over, 'you ain't responsible.'

'I know,' he said.

'If you go singing one of your pub-songs with that girl,' she warned him, 'I see you know about it.'

He cocked his eye at her with purposeful devilishness.

It was late in the evening, just after the May dusk had begun to fall, when my Uncle Silas and Georgina sang their song. My grandmother protested and threatened, not knowing whether she was more disgusted with Silas for enticing the girl or with the girl for making a promise to sing a duet with a man who had been drunk since noon. She retired to the house, excusing herself when she found that the dew was falling. But I stayed outside, in the warm lilac-heavy air, and listened. The guests had been dancing on the grass to the music of two fiddles and a piano brought out of the house. There was a gay atmosphere of laughter and happiness, and besides the fragance of lilac and may-blossom a strange odour of bruised grass and moon-daisies that the dancers had trampled down. My Uncle Silas and Georgina stood at the entrance to the marquee, and Silas took the girl's arm in his and they sang 'I'm Seventeen Come Sunday' without the fiddles or the piano. Uncle Silas had the ugliest voice in the world, and the girl's contralto seemed exquisite beside it. She put an unexpected spirit and passion into her voice:

> 'Will you come to my mammy's house
> When the moon shines bright and clearly?
> And I'll come down and let you in
> And my mammy shall not hear me.'

'Yes,' said my grandmother, who listened after all, from the house, 'and that's what she will do if I know anything.'

All the time my Uncle Silas and Georgina were singing, Abel was watching her. His eyes never flickered or changed their expression of wide, mute adoration. He looked not only as if he would do anything for her, but as if he would forget

or forgive anything she did. He seemed almost stupefied with love and worship of her.

When the song was over my Uncle Silas kissed Georgina with a loud smack. Abel smiled with the serenity of pure adoration, while the guests laughed and applauded. In the silence before the music began for dancing again I could hear the nightingales singing unfrightened in the spinney, and the cuckoos, as in the morning, croaking across the darkening fields in mockery.

It was past midnight when we harnessed the trap and lighted the lamps and my grandfather led the horse down the lane. We could hear my Uncle Silas bawling 'We won't go home till morning' long after we were on the road.

'I'll never come within fifty mile of a wedding with Silas if I live to be a thousand,' my grandmother kept declaring. 'And what in the wide world are you doing, man? Can't you drive straight?'

My grandfather could not drive straight, and my grandmother, reaching suddenly across my sleepy face, took the reins from him and slapped them across the back of the horse.

'Lord, I'd Georgina that girl if she were mine. Kissing Silas!—and he wasn't the only one she kissed, either. Saucy! saucy ain't the word! Somebody's going to be led a fine old dance if I know anything about it. There's going to be trouble afore the year's out.'

But there was no dance and no trouble. Georgina died suddenly, in childbirth, the following spring. My Uncle Silas is dead too. But I shall never forget their song, the girl's spirited loveliness, the feast in the marquee, the smell of lilac and wine and bruised grass, and the sound of the cuckoos contradicting the nightingales.

FINGER WET, FINGER DRY

FINGER WET, FINGER DRY

My Uncle Silas was a man who could eat anything. He could eat stewed nails. He had lived on them, once, for nearly a week. He told me so.

I was a boy then. At that time we used to drive over to see him, in summer, about one Sunday a month, arriving in time for dinner, tethering the white horse about noon in the shade of the big Pearmain overhanging the lane outside. It was always what were we going to eat and what were we going to wet with? At dinner, once, we had pheasant, which was something very special, and I asked him if he had shot it. 'No,' he said, 'it just fell down the chimney.' Another time we had a goose and I asked him if that fell down the chimney. 'No,' he said, 'it was sittin' on eighteen eggs in the winter oats and I cut its two legs off wi' the scythe. Cut 'em off and never broke egg. Ain't that right, George?'

'Yes, that's right,' my grandfather said.

'Well it ain't, then,' Silas said, cocking his bloodshot eye at him. 'Don't you go tellin' the kid such blamed lies. Cut the goose's legs off wi' the scythe!—tck! tck! tck! tck! Don't you believe it, boy. It's just his tale. He's just stuffin' you. The goose went to sleep in the well-bucket and I went to draw some water one night and let it down unbeknownst and it got drowned.'

'Couldn't it swim?' I said.

60

'Oh! it was asleep. Never woke. It just went a belly-flopper and was done for.'

Another time we had venison. I knew what that was. 'A deer,' I said. 'Did that fall down the well?'

'No,' he said. 'I shot it. With a bow and arrow.'

'With what?' I said. 'How?'

'Bow and arrow. One o' these days I'll show you.' And he did. I badgered and bothered him until, one summer Sunday afternoon, he made an ash-bow standing as high as himself and cut arrows out of flower-canes. 'You don't believe me. Do you?' he said. 'Well. I'll show you.' He tipped the arrows with old shoe-awls and bits of filed wire and anything handy. ''Course they ain't no venisons about,' he said. 'But I'll show you.' Then we went into the field beyond the house and Silas stalked an old cow. Finally he stood about ten yards away from her and shot her in the backside. The cow leapt up about ten feet in the air and tore about the field as though she were heat-crazy. 'That's how I done the venison,' Silas said. 'Only it was a bigger bow and a bigger arrow and I hit it a bit harder.'

'Now you know when Silas tells y' anything it's right, don't you?'

'Yes,' I said.

'You know Silas don't tell lies, don't you?' he said. 'You know Silas don't stuff you with any old tale?'

'Yes,' I said. 'I know now.'

It must have been some time after this that he told me the story of the nails, the stewed nails, because it was at some time when I had extra faith in him. I forget how it came up.

Perhaps it was duck eggs; it may have been the sow. I know
he said: 'You kids—blimey, hair and teeth!—you don' know
what it is to go without grub. Look at me. I can eat anything.
Had to. Look at that time I lived on stewed nails for a
week.'

I just stared.

'That's one for you, ain't it? That makes your eyes pop,
don't it? Stewed nails. For a week. And glad to.'

'Didn't they . . . didn't they . . . weren't you bad?' I
said.

'Oh! they was just old nails. I had pepper and salt on
'em, too.'

I asked him how it happened, and when. I remember
having no fear at all that he would tell me. We were alone,
sprawling under the elders beyond the bean-rows, in the
shade. He could tell me anything if we were alone. It was
only in the presence of others that, sometimes, he was not
so sure.

'Oh, about fifty years ago. I was only a kid. About thirty.'
He stopped, eyed me seriously, squinted. 'You ain't goin'
tell nobody about this if I tell you?'

'No. Oh, no!'

'Thass right. There's a policeman at the bottom o' this.
I don't want to git into trouble. You cork it in.'

'I will.'

'Sure? You promise?'

'Finger wet, finger dry,' I said.

'Thass right. And cut *my* throat if I tell a lie. This what
I'm telling y' *is* true.'

He took a quick look round, spoke lower, dropped an eyelid at me, and said: 'I'd gone up to Sam Tilley's to take the old sow to the boar. Sam was a policeman. His wife was a young gal about twenty. She was fiery an' all. Nice gal. I knew her. Sometimes Sam was on night and sometimes he was on days. That time he was on days. Well, it was hot day and after the boar had finished she said: "If you're tired, come in and sit down a bit." So I went in and she said she was tired too. So I made no more to do. "Don't wear a chair out," I said. "Sit on my knee." So she did. She was as light as a chicken, lovely.' He paused, recollecting, licking his loose red lips, going off into a momentary trance. 'Oh! and then—dall it, what happened then? Where was I?'

'She was tired . . . she was resting on your knee,' I said.

'Ah! Thass it. And then . . . oh! I know. We started playing with her duck eggs.'

'What duck eggs?'

'Oh! She kept ducks. Didn't I say that? She had some lovely ducks. And she used to let me have eggs sometimes. I forgot how it was, but we started fooling about with her duck eggs. She kept hiding 'em and I had to find 'em . . . you know. Just fooling about.'

'I know,' I said. 'Like hide the thimble.'

'Thass it. Like hide the thimble. Like that. Only these was duck eggs.'

'Where'd she hide 'em?' I said.

'Oh! In . . . where what? Oh! all over the show. Upstairs,

downstairs. Everywhere. In the oven. In bed. Oh, she was a Tartar. She was hot.'

'With running about so much?'

'Ah, thass it! Running about so much. And then . . .' He looked hard at me, without a twinkle. 'You goin' to cork this in? Keep it secret all right?'

I promised faithfully to cork it in, and he went on:

'Well, then *he* turned up. Sam. All of a sudden she looks out of the window and there he is coming up the garden path. By God, that give me a turn.'

He made motions of a man in a variety of agonies, sweat, thirst, fright, more thirst. I could see he must have been a good deal upset.

'What did you do?' I said.

'Oh! I never done anything. I couldn't. I was scared stiff. It was her who done it. "Here, quick," she says, "in the cellar." And there I was. And there I stopped.'

'How long for?' I said.

'For a week!'

'A week! Why didn't she let you out?'

'She forgot! Forgot all about me. Didn't I tell you how forgetful she was? Oh, she was shocking! Sometimes I'd go up for a dozen duck eggs and she'd bring the boar out and then I'd go for apples and she'd bring me duck eggs. You see?'

'Yes,' I said. 'I see. But why did she lock you in at all? You were all right. You weren't doing anything.'

'Here,' he said. 'You go up to the house and in the corner cupboard you'll see a bottle marked liniment. You bring it.

I want to rub my back. It gives me what'ho! every time I stir.'

So I went to fetch the bottle and after that, for some reason, perhaps because he kept drinking the liniment instead of rubbing his back with it, the tale warmed up. He began to tell me how he lay in the cellar night and day, in complete darkness, not daring to shout out and wondering what would happen to him. But what I wanted to know most was how he had lived—what he had had to eat.

'Eat!' he said. 'Eat? I never had a mossel. Not a mossel. All I'd got was a mite o' pepper and salt screwed up in a mite o' paper in my westcit pocket.'

'You must have got down to skin and bone,' I said.

'Skin and bone . . . you're right,' he said. 'Thass about all I was. And shouldn't have been that if it hadn't been for the nails.'

He went on to tell me, then, how after the third or fourth day, after he had searched every inch of the cellar, floor and ceiling, on his hands and knees, he got so desperate that he began to prize out the nails of the floor boards and how after that there was nothing for it but to eat them and how he made a fire of his pocket linings and splinters of floor board and anything handy and lit it with the only match he had and how he collected water off the damp walls in a tobacco tin and how at last he put the nails in and stewed them.

'Stewed 'em,' he said. 'All one night and all one day. And then ate 'em. I had to. It was either that or snuff it.'

'By golly!' I said. 'What did they taste like?'

''Course it's been a long time ago,' he said. 'They tasted

like . . . oh, I don't know. I had plenty o' pepper and salt on 'em. That took the taste out a bit.'

I sat silent, thinking it over.

''Course it's the iron what done it,' he said. 'Iron's good for you. Ain't it? It was only the iron what done it.'

I still sat silent. It was a fine story, but somehow it seemed, as I sat there in the hot shade of the elders, with their thick, sourish smell rank in the sun, almost too good. I couldn't swallow it. I believed all about the duck eggs and the woman and the cellar and everything—all except the nails. Stewed nails! I kept turning it over in my mind and wondering.

And he must have seen my unbelief. Because suddenly he said:

'You don' believe me now,' he said. 'Do you? You think I'm stuffin' you?'

He looked at me long and hard, with a gaze from which the habitual devilry had been driven out by a marvellous innocence.

'Look at that then.'

He seemed suddenly to have had an inspiration. He opened his mouth, baring his teeth. They were old and broken and stained by the yellow and brown of decay.

'See 'em?' he said. 'That's rust. Nail rust. It got into my teeth.' He spoke with impressive reverence. 'It got into my teeth eating them nails and I never been able to get it out again.'

He gave a sigh, as though burdened with the telling of too much truth.

'That's where women land you,' he said.

A FUNNY THING

A FUNNY THING

My Uncle Silas and my Uncle Cosmo belonged to different worlds; but they were men of identical kidney. Uncle Cosmo was a small man of dapper appearance with waxed moustaches who wore a gold ring on his right hand and a wine-coloured seal on his gold watch-chain, and a green homburg hat. He carried a saucy silver-topped walking-stick and smoked cigars and looked exactly what he was: a masher. If Uncle Silas was the black sheep of one side of the family, Uncle Cosmo was the black sheep of the other. He habitually did an awful thing for which, I think, nobody ever forgave him; he spent his winters abroad. He sent us picture-postcards, then, of orange-trees in Mentone, the bay at Naples, Vesuvius, the gondolas of Venice, of himself in a straw hat on Christmas Day at Pompeii, and wrote, airily: 'On to Greece and Port Said to-morrow, before the final jaunt to Ceylon.' He was reputed, though nobody ever said so, to have a fancy lady in Nice, and there was something about a scandal in Colombo. Returning home in the spring of every year, he brought us oranges fresh from the bough, Sicilian pottery, Oriental cushions, shells from the South Seas, lumps of gold-starred quartz and the war axes of aborginal chieftains, and advice on how to eat spaghetti. He twiddled his seal and told amazing stories of hot geysers on remote southern islands and bananas at twenty a penny and how he had almost fought a duel with a

Prussian in Cairo. Cosmopolitan, debonair, a lady-killer, Uncle Cosmo was altogether very impressive.

The only person not impressed by Cosmo was my Uncle Silas.

'You bin a long way, Cosmo,' he would say, 'but you ain't done much.'

'Who hasn't? I've travelled over half the globe, Silas, while you sit here and grow prize gooseberries.'

'I dare say,' Silas said, 'I dare say. But we only got your word for it. For all we know you might stop the winter in a boardin' house at Brighton.'

'Silas,' Uncle Cosmo said, 'I could tell you stories of places between here and Adelaide that would make your liver turn green. Places——'

'Well, tell us then. Nobody's stoppin' you.'

'I'm telling you. Here's just one thing. There's a desert in Assyria that's never been trodden by the foot of man and that's so far across it would take you three years to cross it on a camel. Now, one day——'

'You ever bin across this desert?'

'No, but——'

'Then how the hell d'ye know it takes three years to cross?'

'Well, it's——'

'What I thought,' Silas said. 'Just what I thought. You *hear* these things, Cosmo, you hear a lot, and you've bin a long way, but you ain't done much. Now take women.'

'Ah!'

'What about this fancy affair in Nice?'

74

'I haven't got a fancy affair in Nice!'

'There you are. Just what I thought. Big talk and nothing doing.'

'She lives in Monte Carlo!'

'Well, that ain't so wonderful.'

His pride wounded, Uncle Cosmo took a deep breath, drank a mouthful of my Uncle Silas's wine as though it were rat poison, pulled his mouth into shape again and said: 'You don't seem to grasp it. It's not only one woman, Silas, in Monte Carlo. There's another in Mentone and another in Marseilles and two in Venice. I've got another who lives in an old palace in Naples, two I can do what I like with in Rome, a Grecian girl in Athens and two little Syrians in Port Said. They all eat out of my hand. Then, there's a niece of a Viscount in Colombo and a Norwegian girl in Singapore, and I forget whether it's four or five French girls in Shanghai. Then, of course, in Japan——'

'Wait a minute,' Silas said. 'I thought you went abroad for your health?'

'Then in Hong Kong there's a Russian girl who's got a tortoise tattooed on her——'

'Well, there ain't nothing wonderful in that, either. Down at 'The Swan' in Harlington there used to be a barmaid with a cuckoo or something tattooed on——'

'Yes, it was a cuckoo,' Uncle Cosmo said. 'I know, because I got her to have it done. She liked me. Yes, it was a cuckoo. And that's why they always used to say you could see the cuckoo earlier in Harlington than anywhere else in England.'

My Uncle Silas was not impressed. He took large sardonic

mouthfuls of wine, cocked his bloodshot eye at the ceiling and looked consistently sceptical, wicked and unaffected. When Uncle Cosmo then proceeded to relate the adventure of the two nuns in Bologna, my Uncle Silas capped it with the adventure of the three Seventh Day Adventists in a bathing hut in Skegness. When Uncle Cosmo told the story of how, in his shirt, he had been held up at the point of a pistol by a French husband in Biarritz, my Uncle Silas brought out the chestnut of how a game keeper had blown his hat off with a double-barrelled gun in Bedfordshire. The higher my Uncle Cosmo flew, the better my Uncle Silas liked it. 'Did I ever tell you,' Uncle Cosmo said, 'of the three weeks I spent in a château in Arles with the wife of a French count?'

'No,' Silas said. 'But did I ever tell you of the month I spent with the duchess's daughter in Stoke Castle? The Hon. Lady Susannah. You can remember her?'

'Well, I—how long ago was this?'

'This was the winter of 'ninety-three. You ought to remember her. She used to ride down to Harlington twice a week, with a groom in a dogcart. Used to wear a black coat with a splashed red lining.'

'Dark girl?'

'That's her. Black. Long black hair and black eyes and long black eyelashes. A dazzler.'

'Well, Silas, now you come to say, I——'

'Now wait a minute, Cosmo. You know what they used to say about this girl?'

'Well——'

'Never looked at a man in her life.' My Uncle Silas went on. 'Never wanted to. Cold as a frog. Nobody couldn't touch her. Chaps had been after her from everywhere—London, all over the place. Never made no difference, Cosmo. She just sat in the castle and looked out of the window and painted pictures. See?'

'Well, I——'

'You know the castle at Stoke? Stands down by the river.'

'Oh, yes, Silas. Very well, very well.'

'The grounds run right down to the river,' Silas said. 'Well, that winter I'd been doing a little river-poaching down there—eel lines and jack-snaring. You know? And about six o'clock one morning I was coming along under the castle wall with about thirty eels in a basket when she copped me.'

'Who?'

'Her. The gal. She was sitting in a gateway in the wall with her easel, painting. It was just gettin' light and she told me afterwards she was painting the dawn over the river. "You been poaching," she said. Well what could I say? I was done. She had me red-handed and she knew it.'

'What did she do?'

'Well, Cosmo, she done a funny thing. She says, "I won't say nothing about this business if you'll come up to the castle and let me paint your picture just as you are. Old clothes and eels and everything." So I says, "It's a go," and we went up to the castle and she began to paint the picture straight away that morning. "The whole family's away abroad for the winter, and I'm all alone here except for the groom and butler," she says. "And after to-day you come along every morning and catch your eels and then come up to the castle and let me paint you."

And my Uncle Silas went on to relate, between wry mouthfuls of wine, how for more than a week he had done as she said, trapping the eels in the early morning and going up to the castle and slipping in by a side door and letting the girl paint him in her room. Until at last something happened. It rained torrentially for a whole day and the succeeding night and when he went down to the river on the following morning he found the floods up and the small stone cattle bridge leading over to the castle smashed by water. It meant a detour of six miles and it was almost eight o'clock by the time he reached the castle. He slipped in by the side door as usual and went upstairs and into the girl's room, and there, standing before a cheval mirror, the girl was painting a picture of herself in the nude.

'And that just about finished it?' Cosmo said.

'No, Cosmo, that just about begun it.'

'Well,' Cosmo said, 'what did she do?'

'A funny thing, Cosmo,' my Uncle Silas said, 'a funny thing. She just went on painting. "I thought you weren't coming," she says, "so I got on with this picture of myself. You like it?" Well, I was standing so as I could see the back of her in the flesh, the sideways of her in the picture and the front of her in the mirror, and I was flummoxed. "Well," she says, "perhaps you don't like it because it isn't finished? Let me put my clothes on and let's have some fried eels and you tell me what you think of it." '

So my Uncle Silas went on to say they had fried eels and talked about the picture and he said something about not being able to judge the picture on such short acquaintance with the model. 'You'll see me again to-morrow,' she said, and so it went on: she painting herself in the nude, Silas watching, until at last, as Silas himself said, a month had gone by and he'd caught almost every eel in the river.

'You heard me say she was cold?' he said. 'Never looked at a man and never wanted one? That's a fairy tale, Cosmo. Don't you believe it. It's true she never looked at men. But she looked at one man. And you know who that was.'

'Yes, but what stopped it?' Cosmo said.

'What stopped it? A funny thing, Cosmo, a funny thing. There were twenty bedrooms in the castle, and we slept in every one of 'em. Then, one night, I was a little fuzzled and I must have gone into the wrong room. As soon as I got in I saw her in bed with another man. She gave one shout. 'My husband!' she says, and I ran like greased lightning and down the drainpipe. The funny thing is she wasn't married, and never was, and I never did find out who the chappie was.'

'You never found out,' Uncle Cosmo said.

'No,' Silas said. 'I never did find out.'

'Well,' Cosmo said, 'it's been a long time ago and I dare say it wouldn't break my heart to tell you. I happen to know, Silas, who that man was.'

'You do?'

'I do.'

'Well,' Silas said, 'who was it?'

Uncle Cosmo took a deep breath and twiddled his waxed moustaches and tried to look at once repentant and triumphant. 'Silas,' he said, 'I hate to say it. I hate it. But that man was me.'

For about a minute my Uncle Silas did not speak. He cocked his eye and looked out of the window; he looked at the wine in his glass; and then finally he looked across at Uncle Cosmo himself.

'Cosmo,' he says at last, 'you bin a long way and you've heard a tidy bit, but you ain't seen much. Don't you know there ain't a castle at Stoke? Nor a river?'

Uncle Cosmo did not speak.

'And don't you know where you was in the winter o' 'ninety-three?'

Uncle Cosmo did not speak.

'Didn't you tell me only yesterday,' Silas said, with his hand on the wine, 'you was in Barbadoes that year, a bit friendly with a bishop's daughter? Now ain't that a funny thing?'

THE SOW AND SILAS

THE SOW AND SILAS

EVERY August, on the Sunday of Nenweald Fair, my Uncle Silas came to visit us. He was a man, sometimes, of strict habits; he wound up his watch after every meal, never let a day pass without a bottle of wine, and never stirred out without his gall-stone, a lump of barbaric rock as large as a pheasant's egg treasured as the relic of an operation at the early age of seventy, carefully wrapped up in a piece of his housekeeper's calico and reverently laid away in the bum-pocket of his breeches.

And in the same strict way he started off early to visit us, spending the whole of Saturday oiling and polishing the harness and grooming the horse, and then another hour on Sunday grooming the horse again and tying his own necktie, all in order to be on the road by eight o'clock. From my Uncle Silas's house to my grandmother's it was less than seven miles; an hour's journey. But somehow, at Souldrop, the horse was tired or my Uncle Silas was tired, and he knew the widow who kept 'The Bell' there; and it seemed a shame to go past the door of the pub itself without going in to take and give a little comfort. And whether it was the giving or the taking of the comfort or what we never knew, but it was nearly eleven o'clock by the time my Uncle Silas drove on to Knotting Fox, where he knew the landlord of 'The George' very well and the barmaid better. From Knotting Fox to Yelden it was less than three miles and at Yelden my Uncle

Silas had a distant relation, a big pink sow of a publican, who had married a second wife as neat as a silk purse. And at Yelden he had no sooner seen the bottom in a quart twice than it was dinner time. 'Stay and have a bit o' dinner now you *are* here,' the little silky woman would say, 'if you don't mind taking it with me while Charlie looks after the bar. We have to take it separate on Sundays.' And my Uncle Silas would consent to stay, almost forgetting to wind up his watch after the dinner in the back parlour with her, and looking like a man on fire when he climbed into the trap at last and drove on to Bromswold, still out of his course, to sit in the bar of 'The Swan' there all afternoon, reverently unwrapping his gall-stone and wrapping it up again for whoever was there to see. 'Feel on it, man. Go on, feel the weight on it. That's a tidy weight y'know. And it used to be bigger, me boyo. Bigger. Used to be bigger'n a duck's egg. What d'ye think o' that? Think of having that inside ye. Eh?'

And all the time, at my grandmother's, we were waiting for him, eating first dinner and then tea without him.

'D'ye reckon Silas ain't coming this year?'

'I'll Silas him if he does!'

'Silas is allus like that there ham. He gets hung up.'

'Yes,' my grandmother would say, 'and that's what I'd *do* with him if I had my way.'

But finally, towards dusk, my Uncle Silas would arrive, lit up, his hat on the back of his head, his face as red as a laying hen's, his neck-tie undone, a pink aster as big as a saucer in his buttonhole, his voice bawling like a bull's to the horse:

'Whoa! Damn you, stan' still. Whoa! George, hold this damn nag still a minute. I wanna git out. Whoa! Stop him.'

'He's bin a'standin' still about five minutes, Silas.'

'Stop him! Whoa. He keeps movin' on and twitterin' about. Stop him! Every 'nation time I try to git out o' this trap he moves on.'

'The nag's as still as a mouse, Silas. You catch hold o' me. You'll be all right. That's it. You catch hold o' me. That's it.'

And somehow my Uncle Silas would alight, waddling across the farmyard on his half-bandy legs like a man on a ship, in gentle staggers of uncertainty, bawling at the top of his devilish voice:

'And now we're here, we *are* here! Whoops! Steady, lost the leg o' me drawers.'

And then in the house: 'Where are y', Tillie, me old duck! Come on, give us a kiss, that's it, give us a kiss. What! Th' old nag lost a shoe. I've bin hung up ever s'long. The old nag lost a——'

'And very lucky you didn't lose yourself, too, I should think!'

'Ah, come on, Tillie, give us a kiss. Silas come all this way and you ain't goin' give him a mite of a kiss?'

'I'd be ashamed of myself!'

'I am.'

'Then just sit down quietly somewhere and don't plague folks and don't act the jabey. George, you get the ham cut and see that there's a knife and fork for everybody and enough bread.'

'After you do that, George, me old beauty, go an' look in the back o' the trap——'

'I recollect I left a few empty bottles under——'

'He'll do no such thing, Silas!'

'God A'mighty, Tillie. God A'mighty, Tillie, they're *empty*.'

'Trust you!'

'Tah! Let 'em *all* come!'

And finally we would sit down to supper, the big dining table and the many little tables crowded with relatives, my grandfather carving the ham and beef, my Uncle Silas staggering round the table and then from one table to another with bottles of cowslip wine, totting it half over the table-cloth, giving an extra stagger of devilry against the ladies, and taking no notice even of my grandmother's tartest reprimands and bawling at the top of his voice:

'Let 'em *all* come!'

'I've said it before and I'll say it again, you shall not come here, Silas, if you can't behave yourself!'

'Let 'em *all* come!'

And bawling constantly, spilling the wine on the floor as he walked, he would get back to his chair at last, only to stagger up again in less than a minute to fill another glass or kiss the lady next to him and show his gall-stone or, worst of all, tell us a story.

'George, me old beauty, d'ye recollect the time as we cut the buttons off old dad Hustwaite's trousers? Remember that, George, me old beauty? Cut 'em off while he sat there in "The Dragon" and then——'

'By golly, Silas, you do——'

'Cut some more ham, George, quick. There's two plates empty.'

'George cut the buttons off while I played him dominoes——'

'Some more *pickle*, Mary Ann?'

And one year, as we sat there eating in the summer half-darkness, the room rich with the smell of ham and beer and the wine my Uncle Silas had spilled wherever he went, and all of us except my grandmother laughing over Silas unwrapping his gall-stone and laying it tenderly in its calico again, my grandfather for some reason got up and went out, and in less than five minutes was back again, with a scared look on his face.

'Silas,' he said. 'Summat's happened. The pig's out.'

'Not the sow, George? The sow ain't out?'

'Busted the door down. How the 'Anover——'

'Let me git up. God A'mighty, let me git up.'

Somehow my Uncle Silas staggered to his feet.

My grandfather and he were men of utterly opposite character, my grandfather as mild as a heifer, Silas as wild as a young colt, but where pigs were concerned they were equal men. Pigs brought out in them the same tender qualities; they gazed in mutual meditation over sty-rails, they suffered from the same outrage and melancholy when their litters failed or their sows were sick. A sow was sacred to them; litters were lovelier than babies.

And my Uncle Silas staggered up as though he were choking.

'My God, let me git out. Let me git out.'

He pushed back his chair, lurched against the table, made an immense effort to right himself, somehow managed to stagger to the door, and then bawled:

'George, boy, she ain't in pig?'

'Yis!' We heard the faint voice far across the farmyard in answer.

'My God!'

The next moment we heard my Uncle Silas slither down all the five stone steps of the back door, blaspheming at every step and blaspheming even more as he sat on his backside in the hen-mucked yard outside. In another moment we heard him blaspheming again as he got to his feet, and still again when he found he could not keep them. By that time all the men in the room were standing up and half the women saying, 'Sit down man, do. All this fuss about a pig!' and some of us were already making for the door.

When I arrived on the threshold, Silas was still sitting in the yard. He seemed to be trying to straighten his legs. He kept taking hold first of one leg, then another. One minute they were crossed and he was trying to uncross them. A minute later they were uncrossed and he seemed to be trying to cross them again.

He saw me coming down the steps.

'Git me up!' he bawled. 'God A'mighty, me legs are tangled like a lot o' wool. Git me up!'

I got hold of him by the shoulders and was getting him to his feet, he staggering and slithering like a man on skates and swearing wildly all the time, when suddenly there was a bawl of alarm from across the yard and I saw the sow come round the straw-stack.

'Silas, stop her, stop her!' my grandfather shouted. 'Head her off, Silas!'

'Git me up, boy, git me up!'

Somehow I managed to get my Uncle Silas to his feet as the sow came blundering across the yard. There was something pathetic about her. She was like a creature in anguish. She was snorting and grunting and slobbering with distress and as my Uncle Silas advanced to meet her he spread out his arms, as though in tender readiness to embrace her.

'Goo' gal, goo' gal,' he kept saying. 'Come on now, tig, tig. Goo' gal. Whoa now!'

Suddenly she saw him. But it was as though she had not seen him. She simply lifted her head and kept straight on. My Uncle Silas too kept straight on, muttering all the time in his thick tender voice: 'Goo' gal, come on now, tig, tig, goo' gal. Tig!' and she snorting and slobbering in the gentle anguish of alarm at her predicament.

All at once my Uncle Silas stopped. He held up his arms and began to leap about with a sort of lugubrious excitement, like a man trying to hold up a train. 'Back, back!' he kept shouting. 'Back. Tig back! Tig!'

But the sow kept straight on. She seemed if anything to increase her pace. And suddenly my Uncle Silas let out a curious yell of blasphemous astonishment and threw up his hands.

The next moment the sow hit him. She caught him full between the legs and she went on after she had struck him, so that momentarily my Uncle Silas was lifted up. For another moment he seemed to ride on the sow's head, backwards, his squat bow legs flapping like the ears of the sow herself. Then the sow threw him. She gave a sort of nodding toss of her head, as a horse does to a fly, my Uncle Silas falling flat on his back in the yard again, his legs waving, his arms clawing wildly at the sow as she stampeded over and past him, her great teats flapping his face and half-smothering his roars of blasphemous rage.

Then something happened. My uncle let out a yell of extreme triumph. The sow stopped. She seemed to stagger, as Silas himself had done, as though her legs were tangled among themselves, and with my Uncle Silas bawling at the top of his voice she gave a sudden sigh and sank on her side.

'George, boy, I got her, I got her! George, I got her!'

'Hold her, hold her!'

'I am holding her! She's atop on me!'

'Hold her for God's sake. Hold her!'

My grandfather came running across the yard and all the men and half the women out of the house. I ran up too.

My Uncle Silas had his arms round the sow's neck. They were locked in embrace, the sow herself was lying over on his chest, her great belly flattened out softly over one of his legs, her teats distended, as though she were about to give suck to a litter.

'I'm holding her, George, I'm holding her.' He spoke with alternate triumph and tenderness. 'Goo' gal, tig, lay still, goo' gal.'

'You hold her a minute, Silas, while we git her up.'

'I'm holding her, George boy. I got her all right.' There was a look of perfect beatitude on my Uncle Silas's face as he lay there with the pig in his arms, a look of pure intoxicated content. 'Goo' gal, tig. I got her, George boy. Tig, tig. Goo' gal!'

'Now Silas'—my grandfather and four men bent over the sow, seizing her great carcase, in readiness to upheave her—'when we lift you let her goo.'

'I got her, George boy, I got her.'

'You let her goo when we lift, Silas.'

'Tig, tig.'

'Now, Silas, now, let goo. Silas, let goo. Dall it, how can we lift her up if you don't let her goo?'

'You wanted me to git her and I got her. Thass all right, ain't it?'

'Yes, Silas, yes. But we can't git her up if you don't let her goo.'

'She's all right. Let her alone. Good old gal, tig, tig.'

'Let goo, Silas, let goo!'

Then the men and my grandfather heaved again, but my Uncle Silas's arms were tight round the sow's neck and the sow herself lay half over him with blissful content, immovable.

'Silas, you must let goo! Now then! Silas! Why the 'Anover don't you let goo! Let goo, Silas, let goo!'

'Thass all right, George boy, thass——'

At that moment my grandmother came up. She was a small, tart, wiry woman, like a bird; her words were like swift pecks at Silas.

'Silas, get up. Get up! Silas, I will not have it. Get up!'

'He won't let goo,' my grandfather said. 'Every time we try to pull the sow off him he won't let goo.'

'Oh, won't he?'

She suddenly seized hold of Silas by the head, just under the neck. From that moment my Uncle Silas lost some of his gaiety and content.

'Tillie, what y'doing on? Let us alone. Tillie, me old——'

'If we can't pull the sow off him we'll pull him off the sow. Get hold of him.'

'It's all right, Tillie. I got her; lemme goo bed with her. I wanna goo bed with her. I wanna——"

'I'd be ashamed of myself, Silas. Stand up!'

Suddenly my grandmother heaved him by the neck and the men heaved too. The sow gave a grunt and a struggle as my Uncle Silas was heaved from beneath her, and in another moment both he and the sow were jerked to their feet, her great teats swinging free and the back buttons of my Uncle Silas's trousers bursting off at the same time like crackers.

'My God, that's done it. Hold 'em up, Silas!'

My Uncle Silas gave a single wild stagger, his trousers falling down, concertina-fashion, before the men caught him and lifted him up and carried him off into the house, his legs windmilling, his wicked devilish voice bawling all over the farmyard above the voices of the shrieking ladies:

'Let 'em *all* come!'

It was the last I saw of him that night. In the morning, when I came downstairs, the guests had gone, my grandfather was in the fields, and there was no one about except my grandmother, who sat in the chair by the kitchen window, sewing the buttons on the back of a pair of tweed breeches.

'Your breakfast's just in the oven,' she said.

For ten minutes I went on eating and she went on sewing, neither of us speaking. Then she bit off her cotton and laid the breeches on a chair.

'When you've finished your breakfast you might take them up to him,' she said. 'Put them down outside the door.'

After breakfast I took the breeches upstairs. I knocked at my Uncle Silas's door, but no one answered. Then I knocked again, but nothing happened, and finally I opened the door a crack and looked in.

'Your breeches,' I said.

My Uncle Silas lay submerged by the bed-clothes. I could see nothing of him but his mouse-coloured hair and a single bleary bloodshot eye which squinted over the coverlet at me.

'Eh?'

'Your breeches.'

'Um.'

After that one utterance he was silent. It was, indeed, all I ever heard him say of his behaviour with the sow, except once, when I reminded him of it over a glass of wine. And then he said:

'What sow? When was that?'

'You remember,' I said. And I told him about it again, laughing as I spoke, telling him how he had caught the sow and held her down and then how the buttons of his breeches had snapped off as we strained to release him.

'You must have been some buttons short that night,' I said. 'Don't you remember?'

He sat silent for a minute, his glass empty in his hand, his lips wet and shining with wine, looking at me with the blandest cocking of his bloodshot eye in an innocent effort of recollection.

At last he shook his head. 'No,' he said. 'There's some things you can't remember.' His hand was on the bottle. 'Mouthful o' wine?'

THE SHOOTING PARTY

THE SHOOTING PARTY

M‌Y Uncle Silas had a small rough paddock with a bramble cowshed at one corner, with two or three acres behind it for corn and potatoes, and one Boxing Day he said to Sammy Twiggle:

'Sammy, Sam boy, there's a couple of pheasants as big as turkeys roost in that ash again my hovel. Come up a New Year's Eve and we'll git the gun. Make a party on it.'

Sammy was a retired house-painter, and he stood about six feet, with arms as long as a monkey's and a face like a laying hen. His nose was bulbous.

My Uncle Silas was no beauty either, with one eye blood-shot and his way of looking cock-eyed and Satanic at the same time. But he could see all right, and so could Sammy. From the tops of ladders, they would say, you got a funny view of the world.

So Sammy came stooping in at Silas's door, like a beery giraffe, about one o'clock on the afternoon of the New Year's Eve, and Silas said: 'Sit down, Sammy, and let's have a wet afore we start. Mouthful o' wine? Tot o' cowslip?'

He filled two tumblers with wine, and then, as they were drinking, he looked hard at Sammy, in wonder. 'What the Hanover's that on top o' your head, Sammy?' he said.

'That?' Sammy said. 'That? That's a shootin' hat.' It was a big, loose green felt with a fancy feather in it.

'Shootin' hat? Looks more like a pair o' the old lady's

hambags dyed green. Shootin' hat. Where'd you git it?'

'You gotta wear a proper hat for shootin',' Sammy said. 'Any fool knows that. This hat belonged to Lord William. It's a real shootin' hat.'

'Is it?' Silas said. 'Well, I'll lay y'a brace o' pheasants to a trousers button it ain't. So there. And I'll tell you what it is. It's a fishin' hat. The pheasants'll think you're a blamed old turkey or summat. A proper shootin' hat's a deer-stalker. Looks like Noah's ark on your head, only upside down. I'll show you. I got one.'

So Silas went upstairs and came down with a check deer-stalker on his head, and Sammy nearly had a fit.

'That? That's a pike-fishin' hat,' he said. 'You undo the flaps and you can sit then all day and your ears don't git cold.'

'Sammy,' Silas said, 'a gent was killed in this hat. Shot at. Mistook for a pigeon. That'll show you whether it's a shootin' hat or not. Look,' he said. 'You see them two little holes this side? Well, that's where the bullets went in. And you see them two little holes that side? That's where·they came out. Drop more wine?'

Silas filled up the tumblers and Sammy, defeated, drank.

'You got the gun loaded?' he said.

'I bin loading it all morning,' Silas said.

The gun was a muzzleloader, about fifty years old, and it was the reason for Sammy and my Uncle Silas coming together. The gun had once belonged to Sammy and my Uncle Silas had bought it from him for fifteen shillings and a young pig on one condition. And the condition was that Sammy should come and shoot with it once a year.

It was a very good gun, except for one thing. There were times when it would not go off. The trigger would jam and nothing on earth would move it. Finally, just as you had given it up as a bad job, it suddenly went off and blew the roof out or killed a cow or something. Otherwise a fine gun.

Silas always loaded it with powder and shot and old news-papers and rusty nails and old rats' nests and hairpins and dried mice and brace-buttons, and, in fact, almost anything lying about, and when it did go off it made a considerable impression.

'Yes, I got him loaded,' Silas said. 'But we can sit a minute. They don't begin to roost until about three o'clock. And, by gosh! Sammy, they're as fat as butter. They're as big as turkeys. I been laying corn down for 'em for over a fortnight. You could catch 'em wi' your hands.'

'Cocks?' Sammy said.

'Cocks. And I tell y' they're as big as turkeys.'

After that they sat still, Silas filling and refilling the glasses, for a long time. It was a cold afternoon, with a light piebald fall of snow on the fields and the air dead still and frozen.

By the time they were on the fourth bottle it was three o'clock, and Sammy said: 'If we don't git started, we shan't see whether they're cocks or hens or bushel baskets.'

'Sammy,' Silas said, 'them pheasants are so tame you could catch 'em in mousetraps. It'll be kids' play. What's wrong wi' sittin' here? Ain't we all right? Another mouthful o' wine?'

So they sat for another half-hour, and the feeling of

twilight, snow-wild, was already growing strong when finally Silas got up and staggered into the kitchen for the gun and the powder-horn and the ramrod and the bag of rusty nails and brace-buttons and odd sweepings up for the reload. 'You carry the bag and the shot, Sammy,' he said. 'I'll carry the gun. And put your hat on straight.'

Very offended, Sammy staggered up, with his hat cocked on the back of his head looking like a cross between a bishop's mitre and a pair of horse's ear-bags. 'Hat's as straight as I am,' he bawled. 'Look at that blamed stag-stalker o' yourn. Terrible.'

'Deer-stalker!' Silas shouted. 'Not stag-stalker. Anyway, it's better'n wearing the old woman's trousers. Pipe down. And let's git on.'

'Shame to leave that drop in the bottle,' Sammy said, 'ain't it?'

'It is, Sammy, it is. Put it in your pocket. Take it with us.'

So Sammy put the wine bottle in his poacher's pocket, and, carrying gun and bags and bottle, they staggered down the garden and over the fence and across the field. In the light snow their tracks made a kind of crazy chain, linking up and staggering away, so that Silas bawled at last: 'What's the use o' me walking straight if you don't? Pull your hat out your eyes, man. How d'ye expect to see straight?'

'Who can't see straight? Eh? Who can't see straight? I'm all right. Where are them pheasants? That's what I wanna know.'

'Sammy boy,' my Uncle Silas said, 'in a minute. All in good time. Whoa. Stand still. You see that hovel?'

'Which one?'

'That one! There's only one!'

'You're a liar. There's two.'

'All right, Sammy. There's two. Now you walk over and behind that hovel and you'll see 'em sittin' on the grass waitin' for you. Two cocks. Eatin' corn. All you gotta do is beat 'em up and I'll have 'em down afore you can wink.'

'All right,' Sammy said. 'Only for God's sake take that blamed stag-stalker off. Else they'll be frit at you.'

'Deer-stalker!' Silas shouted.

Sammy made snake-tracks in the snow. Silas moved after him with dreamy caution. Twilight was deepening with a savage orange light on the horizon beyond the hovel. Suddenly Sammy set up a great shout and the pheasants came over towards my Uncle Silas on fast, dark wings.

Silas took aim, the gun wavering about as though held by a man with St. Vitus's dance, and then shot. The kick of the muzzle-loader knocked him instantaneously flat on his back, and the pheasants veered and swooped and screeched away beyond the house and the spinney and were lost to sight.

'You beat 'em too sharp!' Silas bawled.

'Too sharp be damned!' Sammy shouted. 'That blamed stag-stalker frit 'em to death.'

They stood in the snow, holding each other up, and had a slight offended altercation. It was growing darker. They had a drink. After the shot and the screech of pheasants the day was dead silent. And after the drink they began suddenly to speak in low voices, as though afraid of being heard.

'Sammy, listen to me. You git over th' other side o' that

hedge and go round by Acott's barn and see if you can beat summat up while I git loaded again. There's pheasants run about there like hens. I'll stand under the hedge, so's nobody'll see me. We'll have a couple down in a pop.'

It was almost dark when Sammy climbed the fence, and to Silas, standing under the hedge, the clouds looked like tawny elephants. He stood there for a long time, but nothing happened, and then finally he heard Sammy's voice, in a whisper: 'Ain't you seen it?'

'Seen what?'

'That pheasant. I beat one up as big as a turkey. It walked through.'

'Walked, by golly? I ain't seen a thing.'

'Wait a minute. I'll whistle when it's up.'

In a moment Silas heard a faint whistle like the air escaping from the hole in a barrel, but he could see no bird. He waited, and then Sammy called in a whisper: 'Why don't you shoot?'

'I ain't seen nothing.'

'Then take that stag-stalker off and look. He's sittin' on the fence by the hovel. Pip 'im.'

Silas looked. 'By gum,' he said. 'By gum, if that ain't the biggest pheasant I ever see.'

'Shoot man, shoot afore that blamed hat scares it.'

'Shut up, women's breeches, and let me git aim.'

In the half-darkness Silas took long, slow, unsteady aim at the colossal silhouette of the bird on the fence, and then pulled the trigger. Nothing happened. No sound. And the bird still sat there. In a great sweat of trouble Silas cocked again, took aim, and pulled the trigger. Nothing happened. To Silas the world went round. The great elephant clouds swam tipsily. And still that colossal myth of a bird sat on the fence. Then he cocked a third time and took aim and pulled again. But the gun was dumb.

'Sammy,' he called. 'Sammy boy. She's stuck. Quick, Sam boy, Sammy.'

Sammy fell over the fence, and when he got up again they struggled feverishly, in a sweat of despair, to ease the trigger off. But it was no good. It was as though the thing had frozen. And finally Sammy said: 'It's no use. I'll catch it in me hands. You stop here while I creep up and drop on it. If he gits up and you *can* fire, then fire like blazes.'

Sammy made strange tracks in the snow and finally went behind the hovel, and from that moment my Uncle Silas lost him. All the time he stood trying to ease the gun off, but it was no go.

Then suddenly he looked at the fence and he could see, not one bird, but a brace; two vast dark shapes huddled like roosting turkeys. He began to stagger towards them, stumbling like a man who had seen a vision. It was a sportsman's nightmare; to see, not thirty yards off, a brace of the biggest, and to have, at the same time, a gun that wouldn't go off.

And finally he could bear it no longer. He stopped, took an aim in which the barrel wobbled like a jelly, and then touched the trigger. The gun went off immediately and knocked him flat on his back. It always did that. He expected it, and he was not surprised.

What did surprise him was a sound of moaning. It came from beyond the fence. My Uncle Silas struggled up, rolled across the field like a sailor on the deck of a storm-tossed ship, and found Sammy lying in the ditch, with no hat on, and a fifteen-pound turkey dead on his chest.

'You've killed me,' Sammy said. 'You blowed my hat to bits.'

'Good God, it is a turkey,' Silas said.

'I'm shot,' Sammy said. 'You shot my hat off. I'm done.'

'There was another one. A brace,' Silas said.

'For God's sake,' Sammy said. 'The blood's running down my chest. For God's sake, if it's the last thing you do, git me up.'

So Silas picked up the turkey with one hand and got Sammy up with the other, and it turned out, after a time, that it was not blood running down his chest but wine. Then it seemed that Sammy could stand up, then that he could walk about, and finally that it was not he that was shattered at all, but his hat.

'We gotta find it,' he kept saying, 'we gotta find it.' And at last they did find it, in the next field, in a patch of kale.

'By gum, there's some air-holes in it,' Silas said. 'The old lady'll feel a draught, won't she?'

And the idea was so good and he laughed so much that Sammy wanted to fight him, there and then, in the darkness and the snow.

But two days after New Year's Day he laughed the other side of his face. Sammy's old lady came up then, and gave

him a couple of cracks with a copper-stick that he felt for a month.

For it appears, after all, that she *did* wear that hat. But my Uncle Silas, in revenge, would never have it at all that it was on her head.

SILAS THE GOOD

SILAS THE GOOD

IN a life of ninety-five years, my Uncle Silas found time to try most things, and there was a time when he became a grave-digger.

The churchyard at Solbrook stands a long way outside the village on a little mound of bare land above the river valley.

And there, dressed in a blue shirt and mulatto brown corduroys and a belt that resembled more than anything a length of machine shafting, my Uncle Silas used to dig perhaps a grave a month.

He would work all day there at the blue-brown clay without seeing a soul, with no one for company except crows, the pewits crying over the valley or the robin picking the worms out of the thrown-up earth. Squat, misshapen, wickedly ugly, he looked something like a gargoyle that had dropped off the roof of the little church, something like a brown dwarf who had lived too long after his time and might go on living and digging the graves of others for ever.

He was digging a grave there once on the south side of the churchyard on a sweet, sultry day in May, the grass already long and deep, with strong golden cowslips rising everywhere among the mounds and the gravestones, and bluebells hanging like dark smoke under the creamy waterfalls of hawthorn bloom.

By noon he was fairly well down with the grave, and had

fixed his boards to the sides. The spring had been very dry and cold, but now, in the shelter of the grave, in the strong sun, it seemed like midsummer. It was so good that Silas sat in the bottom of the grave and had his dinner, eating his bread and mutton off the thumb, and washing it down with the cold tea he always carried in a beer-bottle. After eating, he began to feel drowsy, and finally he went to sleep there, at the bottom of the grave, with his wet, ugly mouth drooping open and the beer-bottle in one hand and resting on his knee.

He had been asleep for a quarter of an hour or twenty minutes when he woke up and saw someone standing at the top of the grave, looking down at him. At first he thought it was a woman. Then he saw his mistake. It was a female.

He was too stupefied and surprised to say anything, and the female stood looking down at him, very angry at something, poking holes in the grass with a large umbrella. She was very pale, updrawn and skinny, with a face, as Silas described it, like a turnip lantern with the candle out. She seemed to have size nine boots on and from under her thick black skirt Silas caught a glimpse of an amazing knickerbocker leg, baggy, brown in colour, and about the size of an airship.

He had not time to take another look before she was at him. She waved her umbrella and cawed at him like a crow, attacking him for indolence and irreverence, blasphemy and ignorance.

She wagged her head and stamped one of her feet, and

every time she did so the amazing brown bloomer seemed to slip a little farther down her leg, until Silas felt it would slip off altogether. Finally, she demanded, scraggy neck craning down at him, what did he mean by boozing down there, on holy ground, in a place that should be sacred for the dead?

Now at the best of times it was difficult for my Uncle Silas, with ripe, red lips, one eye bloodshot and bleary, and a nose like a crusty strawberry, not to look like a drunken sailor. But there was only one thing that he drank when he was working, and that was cold tea. It was true that it was always cold tea with whisky in it, but the basis remained, more or less, cold tea.

Silas let the female lecture him for almost five minutes, and then he raised his panama hat and said, 'Good afternoon, ma'am. Ain't the cowslips out nice?'

'Not content with desecrating holy ground,' she said, 'you're intoxicated, too!'

'No, ma'am,' he said, 'I wish I was.'

'Beer!' she said. 'Couldn't you leave the beer alone in here, of all places?'

Silas held up the beer-bottle. 'Ma'am,' he said, 'what's in here wouldn't harm a fly. It wouldn't harm you.'

'It is responsible for the ruin of thousands of homes all over England!' she said.

'Cold tea,' Silas said.

Giving a little sort of snort she stamped her foot and the bloomer-leg jerked down a little lower. 'Cold tea!'

'Yes, ma'am. Cold tea.' Silas unscrewed the bottle and

held it up to her. 'Go on, ma'am, try it. Try it if you don't believe me.'

'Thank you. Not out of that bottle.'

'All right. I got a cup,' Silas said. He looked in his dinner basket and found an enamel cup. He filled it with tea and held it up to her. 'Go on, ma'am, try it. Try it. It won't hurt you.'

'Well!' she said, and she reached down for the cup. She took it and touched her thin bony lips to it. 'Well, it's certainly some sort of tea.'

'Just ordinary tea, ma'am,' Silas said. 'Made this morning. You ain't drinking it. Take a good drink.'

She took a real drink then, washing it round her mouth.

'Refreshin', ain't it?' Silas said.

'Yes,' she said, 'it's very refreshing.'

'Drink it up,' he said. 'Have a drop more. I bet you've walked a tidy step?'

'Yes,' she said, 'I'm afraid I have. All the way from Bedford. Rather farther than I thought. I'm not so young as I used to be.'

'Pah!' Silas said. 'Young? You look twenty.' He took his coat and spread it on the new earth above the grave. 'Sit down and rest yourself, ma'am. Sit down and look at the cowslips.'

Rather to his surprise, she sat down. She took another drink of the tea and said, 'I think I'll unpin my hat.' She took off her hat and held it in her lap.

'Young?' Silas said. 'Ma'am, you're just a chicken. Wait

till you're as old as me and then you can begin to talk. I can remember the Crimea!'

'Indeed?' she said. 'You must have had a full and varied life.'

'Yes, ma'am.'

She smiled thinly, for the first time. 'I am sorry I spoke as I did. It upset me to think of anyone drinking in this place.'

'That's all right, ma'am,' Silas said. 'That's all right. I ain't touched a drop for years. Used to, ma'am. Bin a regular sinner.'

Old Silas reached up to her with the bottle and said, 'Have some more, ma'am,' and she held down the cup and filled it up again. 'Thank you,' she said. She looked quite pleasant now, softened by the tea and the smell of cowslips and the sun on her bare head. The bloomer-leg had disappeared and somehow she stopped looking like a female and became a woman.

'But you've reformed now?' she said.

'Yes, ma'am,' Silas said, with a slight shake of his head, as though he were a man in genuine sorrow. 'Yes, ma'am. I've reformed.'

'It was a long fight?'

'A long fight, ma'am? I should say it was, ma'am. A devil of a long fight.' He raised his panama hat a little. 'Beg pardon, ma'am. That's another thing I'm fighting against. The language.'

'And the drink,' she said, 'how far back does that go?'

'Well, ma'am,' Silas said, settling back in the grave, where he had been sitting all that time, 'I was born in the hungry 'forties. Bad times, ma'am, very bad times. We was fed on barley pap, ma'am, if you ever heard talk of barley pap. And the water was bad, too, ma'am. Very bad. Outbreaks of smallpox and typhoid and all that. So we had beer, ma'am. Everybody had beer. The babies had beer. So you see, ma'am,' Silias said, 'I've been fighting against it for eighty years and more. All my puff.'

'And now you've conquered it?'

'Yes, ma'am,' said my Uncle Silas, who had drunk more in eighty years than would keep a water-mill turning, 'I've conquered it.' He held up the beer-bottle. 'Nothing but cold tea. You'll have some more cold tea, ma'am, won't you?'

'It's very kind of you,' she said.

So Silas poured out another cup of the cold tea and she sat on the graveside and sipped it in the sunshine, becoming all the time more and more human.

'And no wonder,' as Silas would say to me afterwards, 'seeing it was still the winter ration we were drinking. You see, I had a summer ration with only a nip of whisky in it, and then I had a winter ration wi' pretty nigh a mugful in it. The weather had been cold up to that day and I hadn't bothered to knock the winter ration off.'

They sat there for about another half an hour, drinking the cold tea, and during that time there was nothing she did not hear about my Uncle Silas's life: not only how he had re-formed on the beer and was trying to reform on the language but how he had long since reformed on the ladies and the horses and the doubtful stories and the lying and everything else that a man can reform on.

Indeed, as he finally climbed up out of the grave to shake hands with her and say good afternoon, she must have got the impression that he was a kind of ascetic lay brother.

Except that her face was very flushed, she walked away with much the same dignity as she had come. There was only one thing that spoiled it. The amazing bloomer-leg had come down again, and Silas could not resist it.

'Excuse me, ma'am,' he called after her, 'but you're liable to lose your knickerbockers.'

She turned and gave a dignified smile and then a quick, saucy kind of hitch to her skirt, and the bloomer-leg went up, as Silas himself said, as sharp as a blind in a shop-window.

That was the last he ever saw of her. But that afternoon, on the 2.45 up-train out of Solbrook, there was a woman with a large umbrella in one hand and a bunch of cowslips in the other. In the warm, crowded carriage there was a smell of something stronger than cold tea, and it was clear to everyone that one of her garments was not in its proper place. She appeared to be a little excited, and to everybody's embarrassment she talked a great deal.

Her subject was someone she had met that afternoon.

'A good man,' she told them. 'A good man.'

A HAPPY MAN

A HAPPY MAN

THERE were many sides to the character of my Uncle Silas which were very doubtful; but there was nothing doubtful about his friendship with Walter Hawthorn.

Walter and Silas had been friends for fifty or sixty or perhaps even seventy years, though for more than half that time they had never seen each other. Walter had been a soldier: long periods of service on the North-West Frontier, the Sudan, garrison at Singapore.

He was a big man, with huge sun-dark hands, massive shoulders as stiff and square as iron brackets. He had been wounded twice on the Frontier and once in the Sudan, but he never talked about it. They had given him medals for conspicuous gallantry in a tribal ambush in Afghanistan and others for long service and distinguished service, and he had a row of ribbons that was like a section out of a rainbow. But he never wore the medals or the ribbons and when folks tried to get him to talk about his campaigns and his bravery he would just say, 'Yes, that was in '79. It was bad,' or 'Yes, that was in '84. That was the day.'

He was a man who had seen things and done things and had helped to make history, but it was as though he had done nothing at all. There are men who go round the world and see all there is to be seen and who come back and say, 'It was very nice indeed.'

Walt Hawthorn was one of these men. Except that when

he came home, after more than forty years of service, he didn't even say that. He said nothing at all, and settled down to grow flowers.

It was not the fact that he grew flowers that was in any way remarkable: it was the kind of flowers he grew. My Uncle Silas also grew flowers. He had always been an ugly little man, and it was as though the littleness and ugliness in him demanded to be expressed in something huge and wonderful.

His dahlias were like grand velvet cushions of salmon and scarlet, his asters like ostrich plumes of pink and mauve. He gloried in sprays of monster golden lilies that were like the brasses in an orchestra. He liked roses into which he could bury his face.

But Walt Hawthorn was fond of little flowers. His garden was at the other end of the lane from my Uncle Silas, and the two gardens were like the plus and minus of things. Where my Uncle Silas's flowers flaunted and flared over the hedge in the sun, Walt Hawthorn had scarcely a flower that could look over the fence.

In spring he grew things like forget-me-nots and violets and narcissi and Dresden daisies; in summer he had virginia stock and snapdragons and pinks and button asters. When he went to my Uncle Silas's garden my Uncle Silas would take a yardstick to the dahlias, but when Silas went to see Walt Hawthorn, Walt would take him to see a rose no bigger than a thimble or his six-inch fuchsia, in a pot, with flowers no bigger than a pendant ear-ring.

They went on like this for years. It seemed to consolidate

their friendship. With other men my Uncle Silas boasted of his flowers as he boasted of his women, or he lied of one as easily as he lied of the other. But he never boasted to Walt Hawthorn, and, except for one simple occasion, he never lied.

Walt Hawthorn and my Uncle Silas, though they differed in almost every other way, were alike on one thing. They liked a drink about midday. And every day, just before twelve o'clock, they walked down to 'The Swan with Two Nicks' and, without fail, they drank the same thing: a pint of draught ale.

One day when my Uncle Silas shouted: 'Ready, Walt?' over the fence it was three or four minutes before Walt Hawthorn appeared. It was a blinding hot day in July, the crest of a heat wave that had been rising for almost a week, and when Walt appeared my Uncle Silas noticed a curious, unusual thing about him. He was wearing a bunch of flowers in his buttonhole.

Normally, beside my Uncle Silas, Walt Hawthorn looked like a man on stilts; but that day, as they walked down the road in the blazing sunshine, it seemed to Silas that Walt had shrunk a little. The brackets of his shoulders seemed to have bent down a little. His feet kept scraping the ground.

My Uncle Silas looked at the flowers in his buttonhole. 'Toffed up a bit?' he said.

'Ah,' Walter said. His eyes were fixed on the distance. 'Got me medals on.'

Silas did not take much notice of that remark. He took it

for a kind of joke. He did not take much notice of the next remark either.

'Don't walk so fast, general,' Walt said.

The reason Silas did not take much notice of this remark was because there were odd times when Walt Hawthorn did call him 'general.' What he noticed was that Walt was walking very slowly.

Silas noticed this all the way to the pub and all the way back, and he noticed it even more the following day. It was hotter than ever that day, and Walt had a bigger bunch of flowers in his buttonhole.

'Got your medals on again?' Silas said.

'Yes,' Walt said, and suddenly he took one of the flowers, a pansy, and put it in Silas's buttonhole.

Silas did not say anything. There was nothing very odd after all in putting a flower in the buttonhole of a friend. But when they reached the pub something else happened.

Walter began to take all the flowers out of his own coat and put them into Silas's buttonholes—not only the buttonholes of his coat but the buttonholes of his waistcoat and then the buttonholes of his trousers. The large sun-browned hands moved very gently. They handled the little virginia stocks and pansies and pinks, limp now from sun, with crazy affection. My Uncle Silas did not say anything, but as he sat there, letting the flowers be threaded foolishly and lovingly into his garments, he felt that he saw a big man growing little before his eyes.

He saw the eyes of a big man who had seen the world and

had helped to hammer out its history becoming the eyes of a child who has seen nothing and wants to do nothing better than play with a handful of flowers.

Gradually Silas got Walter Hawthorn out into the sun again and began to lead him home. For a time they walked very slowly. Suddenly Walter leapt into the air and slid down into the ditch by the roadside, pulling Silas with him, and began to fire at rebel tribesmen on the North-West Frontier.

It was then that my Uncle Silas began to tell lies to Walter Hawthorn. He told him lies about everything: the dead, the living, the way the fight was going. After the skirmish was over he got Walter back to his house and then told more lies. Yes, there was plenty of ammunition. Yes, the general was here. Then Walter began to point to the flowers in the garden, raving. 'See 'em?' he yelled. 'See 'em? See 'em, general?' and Silas got ready to lie about them, too, thinking that perhaps Walter saw them as soldiers. But Walter leapt up in crazy terror. 'It's a mirage!' he shouted. 'It's a bloody mirage.'

Soon after that he became quieter. He sat in the kitchen, in the cool, out of the sun, and Silas gave him a little whisky and water. Then Silas got him to lie down on the sofa, and after that he went home.

It was less than two hours when Silas went back to him. When he went into the garden, in the dead still heat of the afternoon, he was dumbfounded. The flowers had been pulled up everywhere; they were strewn over the paths and the grass and the steps of the house and in the house itself.

They had been clawed up by the desperate savagery of a man who sees a mirage and wants to grasp it before it vanishes, and Walter himself was lying down among them, exhausted, like a man who had fought all his campaigns in a single afternoon.

Later that evening they fetched him in an old-fashioned limousine with black bobbed curtains that could be drawn over the windows. He was quite quiet and gentle and Silas helped to lead him out of the house. In his huge feeble hands he held large bunches of little flowers.

'Well, general,' he said to Silas, 'where are we bound for this time? India?'

'India it is,' Silas said.

He stood in the road and watched the limousine depart. As it went down the road he saw one of Walter Hawthorn's huge hands come out of the window. The hand flung flowers on to the road, and in that moment it seemed to my Uncle Silas that Walter Hawthorn was a happy man.

SILAS AND GOLIATH

SILAS AND GOLIATH

WHEN I was a little boy my Uncle Silas used to tell me about a man named Porky Sanders, and how he knocked him into Kingdom Come.

'Porky the Gorilla they used to call him,' he would say, 'and he was champion o' the world.'

'A boxer?'

'A boxer?' my Uncle Silas would say with great derision. 'Boxing wasn't heard on. I'm talking about the days o' prize fights. I'm talking about the days when you chewed a man's ear off if you didn't like his whiskers.'

'Did you ever chew a man's ear off?' I would say.

'Boy,' he would say to me with great solemnity, 'I was the champion ear-chewer of the county.'

Then he would go on to tell me that it was about the year 1870. 'The year the horned wheat stood nearly ten feet high in Deanes' forty acre, at the bottom of the lane. I ain't kiddin' you. Everything was bigger in them days.

'Take a man,' he would say, 'like Porky. At the time I'm tellin' y' about, Porky stood six foot six and weighed about twenty stone. He could hold six beer-glasses in the palm of his hand. Yes, boy. And two men could stand in one leg of his trousers. Yes!' he would say, 'all the best men were big men in them days.'

'But you were a little man,' I would say.

My Uncle Silas would look at me with a deadly serious cock of one eye, with the bland, sly darkness that he always kept for awkward moments and awkward questions.

'Yes, boy. Yes, I was a little man,' he would say. 'But I always had a big head.'

After that my Uncle Silas would go on to describe not only how big Porky Sanders was and how famous he was, but what a smashing, hell-fire, holy terror he was. It was not simply that he was a man who fought: it was not only that he was a man who bit off other men's ears. It seemed that he was a kind of dictator who walked about crushing other men under his foot like beetles.

He walked into public-houses and bounced beer-barrels; and if the landlord didn't like it, he would, my Uncle Silas said, bounce the landlord. If he fancied an apple, he clawed branches of apples from over a garden wall as he passed; if he wanted a leg of mutton, he walked into the butcher's shop and grabbed the meat with one hand and belted the butcher with the other, and then walked out of the shop gnawing the raw meat like a toffee-apple.

If he fancied a girl he picked her up and walked away with her under his arm, more or less, like a prize puppy. He drank a gallon of beer at a time, and when he walked down the street the women went indoors and the men all got together in a bunch for safety.

Did I know a man named Sip Turner, my Uncle Silas said, a man with a nose that looked like a corkscrew? Well, that was some of Porky Sanders's work. Porky had picked up the man by the nose and spun him round like a Catherine

wheel, one day in '69, because he wouldn't call him 'sir.'
That's the kind of man he was, Silas said, the biggest belch-
ing blustering blackguard in the county. A real gorilla.

'And why,' I would want to know, 'did they call him a
gorilla?'

My Uncle Silas had an answer for everything. 'Been a
sailor,' he said. 'Been a sailor and got marooned for eighteen
months on an island off the cost of Africa, and all that time
never ate nothing but gorilla meat. Don't you see,' he said.
'That's what made him so strong?'

And so gradually I got fixed in my mind the awful, blood-
thirsty, terrifying picture of the flesh-eating, ear-chewing,
woman-grabbing Porky Sanders. The only thing that began
to trouble me was how my Uncle Silas had knocked him into
Kingdom Come.

'I am coming to that,' he would say. 'I am coming to that.
You see, it was like this. There was a lady. A great friend of
mine. Vicky her name was. And one day Porky picked
her up.'

Here my Uncle Silas would pause with great significance,
as though this had been one of the fundamental moments in
history. 'And that,' he would say, 'is where he made a very
great mistake.'

'I bet you challenged him?' I said.

'Yes,' my Uncle Silas would say. 'Yes, boy, I challenged
him. Raw fists. Any time. Any place. Every knock-down a
round. Fight to go on until one man couldn't get up no
more. Yes, I challenged him—and he laughed at it. Laughed
fit to bust himself.'

I asked what happened then.

'I just let him laugh, boy,' he said, 'and then got to work. You see, Vicky didn't like being picked up by that gorilla any more than any other girl. She hated it like poison, but she couldn't do nothing. So I got on to her first. "Vicky," I says to her, "play on his pride." '

And then he would go on to tell me how the girl had played on his pride, asking him if he was afraid of a little bit of a winkle like Silas, telling him how people were saying he was afraid, and urging him to cut Silas up, once and for all, into sausage meat. She kept at him for days, and at last it worked. 'Then,' Silas said, 'I got her to feed him on cucumbers. You see, it was hot weather. And she'd say to him, "Porky dear, you got to keep your blood cool. Porky dear, the best thing in the world you can eat is cucumbers." And she got round him on that, too, and somehow she kept him on nothing but cucumbers for a fortnight.

'Cucumbers and beer,' he said, and then went on to tell me how he worked with the landlord at the pub, too: how the beer would be free for Porky every night and not only how it would be free, but how every pint had been specially jiggered behind the bar: a spoonful of salts in it, a pill or two, a packet of something from the chemist's, things that turned his stomach to fire and water.

'So that in the end,' my Uncle Silas said, 'what with the bellyache from the beer and the bellyache from the cucumbers, Porky turned up for the fight looking as green as a boiled frog.'

'And all you had to do,' I said, 'was lick him with one hand.'

'Better than that,' my Uncle Silas said, with great modesty. 'Better than that. I licked him with no hands at all.'

There was always a moment in my Uncle Silas's stories when something or other seemed too good to be true, and this, it seemed to me, was such a moment.

Uncle Silas must have seen the doubt rising in my eyes, for a moment later he went on:

'Boy, didn't I tell you I was a little man, but I had a big head? Well, I didn't tell you that for nothing!' He cocked his bloodshot eye at me with swift, diabolical wickedness. 'The fight was down on Vine Hills,' he went on, 'you know—under the wood, just before you get to that big slope.'

'Near the river?' I said.

'Near the river,' he said, and then he went on to tell me how it had happened: how all he did was to clutch the gorilla by the waist and bunt his head into a stomach tired and weak already from beer and purges and cucumbers, and how at first it was a kind of standstill bunting, then a run and a bunt, and then a charge and a bunt, every bunt producing a low, agonized, sour sort of groan.

Finally, I got a picture of my Uncle Silas standing halfway across the field, and Porky being held up by the thick excited crowd, and my Uncle Silas bearing down on him with a sort of charge of the Light Brigade, Porky being driven inexorably farther and farther down the slope until at last, with a triumphant and masterful bunt, my Uncle

Silas put him with a sort of inverted belly-flopper into the river.

At the end of it my Uncle Silas would gaze airily about him with extreme modesty. 'Yes, that's how,' he would say, 'I knocked Porky Sanders into Kingdom Come.'

'Is it?' a voice would say.

And we would turn to see, as always at the conclusion of some riper, more racy tale, my Uncle Silas's housekeeper in the room; tart, irascible, iron-eyed, disgusted. 'Well, if it is,' she would say, 'I'd be ashamed. I'd be ashamed I would. Telling the boy such downright nonsense and such tales about things that never happened.'

For a minute my Uncle Silas, sardonic and unruffled, would retain a kind of apostolic composure.

Then he would speak. 'Tales?' he would say. 'I don't see no difference in telling a tale like that and telling a tale about a woman turning into a pillar o' salt, or a man who was alive for three days in a fish's belly.'

And now that I come to think of it, nor do I.

A SILAS IDYLL

A SILAS IDYLL

'THE world,' my Uncle Silas used to say, 'looks different from the top of a ladder.' It was a remark based on years of experience, for in the 'sixties and 'seventies my Uncle Silas had been a thatcher.

It was a good trade, with plenty to do, and as time went on my Uncle Silas bought himself a little beer-coloured nag and a little flat two-wheeled cart, and drove himself for twenty or thirty miles out and about the countryside, thatching barns and houses, stacks, and lych-gates.

He could cling to the side of a house in a March wind like a monkey, and there was no one like him for combing out the thatch until it was as smooth as a girl's hair or trimming a rippled eave to the line of a scallop-shell.

In an age of thatchers he was a master, and, like all masters, he signed his work. His signature was a cockerel. With a comb like a newt and a tail like a fan of barley and looking altogether flamboyant and triumphant about some-thing, this cockerel was twisted out of straw and fixed to gable and stack-top and barn-roof wherever my Uncle Silas went.

It was a sign that became in time as well known as a barber's pole, and in time, too, it gave rise to a sort of proverb. 'When the cockerel's about,' they said, 'let the hens look out.'

One day my Uncle Silas was thatching a shop-roof down in Bedford. On the lower floor of the shop you could buy ribbons and calico, dress materials and hats; on the upper floor there were twenty little dressmakers working under a supervisor, who looked, as my Uncle Silas said, as if her bosom was made of mangel-wurzels and her heart of crab apples. She was very fair, solid and suspicious.

Every time he went up the ladder with a load of straw or pegs she clucked like an old hen with chickens. Every time he came down again she would be standing at the window, spread out, hiding the chickens behind her. All the time, my Uncle Silas said, she looked as red as if she was going to lay an egg.

A mourning order had come in; everyone was working against time. The girls were pretending to be very serious, as if damped down by death, and they had not time to look at him.

All except one. She was a little brown creature sitting near the window, and every time Silas went up or down the ladder she lifted her head and grinned at him. Her hair was a brownish-red shade, and it crinkled and fluffed like hens' feathers.

Once when he came up the ladder the window was open enough for him to speak to her. 'Nice day,' he said.

'Very.'

That was all she said. But it almost made my Uncle Silas swoon off the ladder. It had a tender, intoxicating sound that turned his legs to water. When he came down again he said:

'When does old turnip-face go home for dinner?'

'Doesn't go. Has dinner here.'

'When do you go?' he said.

'Don't go. Have my dinner here, too.'

As he went down the latter he heard the old turnip's voice snap out: 'Less looking out of the window, Elizabeth, and more concentration on your work. I've to take these dresses to be fitted at two o'clock.'

At five minutes to two my Uncle Silas saw the old turnip-faced supervisor come out of the shop with a large brown-paper parcel under her arm; at two o'clock precisely he was up the ladder, giving a sort of cockadoodledoo to the girls through the window; at ten minutes past two he had climbed through the window and was properly playing the cockerel in the hen-roost.

The girls fluttered and twittered, and it wasn't long before he was plaiting a love-knot with some odd strands of straw for the little brown-haired creature who had been sitting near the window.

She was so sweet and attractive that he forgot all about the thatching, and the girls, it seems, forgot all about the supervisor. My Uncle Silas was just beginning to plait love-knots for each of the twenty dressmakers on a sort of barter system, no kiss, no love-knot, when one of the girls, who had been downstairs to fetch a length of velvet, rushed excitedly into the room, slammed the door and said the supervisor was coming back upstairs.

Even as she spoke they could hear the clump of her feet on the stairs and in the ten clear seconds that followed there was nothing for it but to clap my Uncle Silas, like Falstaff, into the nearest linen basket.

And from there, looking through the wickerwork, he saw the supervisor come in. She flounced in, put down the parcel in a great hurry and proceeded to tell twenty innocent-looking girls, half of them hiding love-knots to their bosoms, why she was back so soon.

It was the age of tight-lacing, fainting-fits and general feminine hysteria in the face of catastrophe, and it seemed that the mother and daughter for whom the mourning dresses had been made were in a state of prostrate hysterics and could not be fitted.

'Which is why,' the supervisor said, 'I had to come back. The mother is about my size and the daughter is about the size of one of you. We'll have to fit them as best we can. Fanny, unpack the parcel. Lucy, help me off with my dress.'

Well, as my Uncle Silas said, the world looks different from up a ladder, but it's nothing to how different it looks through the cracks in a linen-basket.

'I always thought the Rock of Gibraltar was well fortified,' he would say. 'But it was nothing to the fortifications old turnip-face had on. She'd got more whale-bone than a whale. Talk about the Siege of Ladysmith. It was nothing. She could have held out for a century. Even her legs were in sandbags.'

'Elizabeth,' the supervisor said, 'slip off your dress and just try the other one on.'

As she spoke, a sort of tittering rustle of feathers went through the twenty dressmakers; my Uncle Silas stuffed bits of dress material into his mouth to keep from having hysterics himself, and a moment later he was looking at the nicest array of pale pink petticoats he had ever set eyes on.

'Yes,' he said, 'pink petticoats. And fifty years ago that meant something.'

And then he would go on to tell me how he had remained a prisoner in the linen basket all that afternoon, taking his alternate review of, as he said, fortifications and fancy-work, until his body was cramped and stiff and even his heart had pins-and-needles.

And it was his heart, it seems, that went on having pins-and-needles for a long time afterwards, for when he finally got out of the basket late that evening, after the shop was closed and the girls had gone, he climbed down the ladder and almost fell into the arms of the little brown-featured creature waiting for him at the bottom with a straw love-knot pinned at her neck.

'And what happened?' I said. 'What did you do?'

'Boy,' he said, 'I did the only thing you could do in them days when you'd seen a lady in her petticoats.'

'And what was that?'

'I married her,' he said. 'She'd have been your aunt if she'd lived.'

And as he spoke there would come into my Uncle Silas's eye an expression not often seen there. It was soft, distant, regretful, and indescribably tender. It transfixed him for one moment and then he became his old sardonic self again.

'Yes,' he would say, 'they say when the cat's away the mice'll play. But it's nothing to what the hens'll do when the cockerel pops in the roost.'

THE RACE

THE RACE

Goffy Windsor was a tall, streaky fellow with a horse-face and legs like ostrich's, who boasted he could run a mile in five minutes.

My Uncle Silas, who had legs that wouldn't have stopped a pig in an entry and who never, of course, boasted about anything, used to tell how he challenged Goffy to a five-mile race, and beat him to a frazzle.

There are many men like Goffy Windsor. When they are young men they win bets for drinking a quart straight off; they hit cricket balls for six; they floor the board at skittles five times running; they run a mile in five minutes.

No one has much to say about this. But gradually, as they grow older, they begin to recall how they drank a gallon straight off for ten nights running, how they hit a cricket ball over a church steeple and killed a chicken stone dead on the other side; how they used to be able to floor the skittle board six times out of six, blind-folded, left-handed, upside down, and throwing between their legs; and finally, how they knicked five seconds off the mile-time for the world's record in 1889, easy as shelling peas, only it was never official.

It was like this with Goffy Windsor. Whenever there was a crowd of strangers in 'The Swan with Two Nicks' on a Saturday night, Goffy would begin to demonstrate the kidney punch he used for knocking out the welter-weight of Great Britain and Ireland in 1891—'Of course the kidney

punch is barred now,' he'd say—or the under-arm break that made a ball come in two feet six and bowl Georgie Colson, the county man, in 1894—'only, of course, they bowl over-arm nowadays'—or the famous occasion when he did the mile in 4 minutes 59.3 secs. on a practice run—'and old Charley Taylor would tell you it was right, too,' he'd say, 'only Charley's dead.'

One night Goffy was telling a young man in a fancy pullover how he once raced against all-comers at the Crystal Palace and left them standing, when my Uncle Silas interrupted.

'Goffy,' he said, 'you were a 'nation good miler. But anything over a mile and you were poor stuff. Why, I'd lick you myself.'

'Don't talk wet,' Goffy said.

'I ain't talking wet,' Silas said, 'I'm challenging you. If this gentleman here likes to put up a bit of a side-stake I'll race you for five miles any day. When and where you like.'

'That's fine,' the young man said. 'I'll put up a couple o' quid stake. Go on.'

So they settled it there and then that Goffy and Silas should run a race in three weeks' time, on a Sunday morning, between Carlton and Solbrook, on the top road above the river.

'I don't want to be hard on you, Silas,' Goffy said. 'So I'll give you a mile start.'

'No,' Silas said. 'But I'll tell you what. You can give me five minutes' start. All right?'

'Anything you like,' Goffy said.

'And everybody off the track. No bikes. Nobody. That all right?'

'Anything you like,' Goffy said.

They shook hands on it and the young man in the pullover put down his money with the landlord, and the next day Goffy went into training. He put on a sweater and rubber shoes and trotted through the village every morning. In the evenings, at the pub, he drank ginger ale and slapped his chest and let all-comers feel how his legs were coming on.

All the time my Uncle Silas did not do anything. He did not go into training and he could see no sense in drinking ginger ale. He did not boast at all, but three days later he gave out that he couldn't sleep at nights for sciatica.

'Sciatica?' they said. 'That ain't much good for running, is it?'

'No,' he said. 'No. And I get cramp too. Chronic.'

By that time everybody was talking about the race and there was already a lot of money on it, too. When the word went round that my Uncle Silas wasn't training and that he was suffering from cramp and sciatica the odds against him lengthened to 10 to 1.

That night he talked it over with Walter Hawthorn, and the next day Walter gave it out that Silas was suffering from a strained groin and rheumatics in the knee joint, and one or two other minor ailments, like gum-boils.

Altogether everybody thought that Silas was in a very poor way indeed, and that day Walter Hawthorn got a lot of money on him at 20 to 1. The night before the race Uncle Silas threw a fit, so next morning the starting price was 33 to 1.

The race was due to start at ten o'clock from 'The King's Head' in Carlton. Goffy turned up looking like an ostrich in white drawers, and did a lot of fancy exercises, loosening-up, in front of the pub. My Uncle Silas was in just his shirt and trousers and a pair of rubber shoes, and had an ash-bough in his hand to keep the flies away.

At ten o'clock my Uncle Silas went trotting off, looking just like a squat little pig that can't and won't be hurried.

My Uncle Silas trotted on for five minutes and then calmly lay down in the middle of the road. He lay there for a few minutes, fairly comfortable, resting, getting his wind back, and then Goffy came ostriching out of the distance, wheezing like a harmonium.

Goffy hadn't then got his second wind, and he was trying to go very hard when he saw Silas lying flat in the road as if he were dead.

He bent over my Uncle Silas. 'Silas,' he said, 'are you all right? Y'aint done for?'

My Uncle Silas, who was lying on his back, gave a groan somewhere between a bellyache and the sound of a priest intoning for a lost soul.

'Can I do anythink, Silas?' Goffy said. 'Can I do anythink?'

'In my hip-pocket,' Silas whispered. 'There's a bottle in me hip-pocket.'

Goffy lifted Silas upright, and then found the bottle and put it to Silas's lips. 'What is it, Silas?' he said.

'Whisky,' Silas said in a slobbing sort of voice. 'Have a drop.'

By this time Goffy was feeling badly about things. He

kept thinking about Silas's sciatica and rheumatics and the fit he had thrown, and he took a long, sudden drink of whisky to steady himself.

'Goffy,' my Uncle Silas said, 'it might be the last time I shall see you. If it is, I want you know you ain't to blame.'

Goffy, who had eaten nothing since six o'clock that morning, and had drunk nothing stronger than ginger ale for a fortnight, took another smack at the whisky.

'You think you can carry me to the house back there?' Silas said. 'Carry me if you can, Goffy.'

Goffy looked up and saw a house about half a mile back along the road. His heart sank. 'It's too far,' he said. 'But I'll run back. I'll run back as quick as I can and get somebody.' Then he took another swig at the whisky and pelted back along the road.

My Uncle Silas let him get safely round the first bend in the road and then he got up and trotted steadily on. He knew that he had almost a mile start and he knew something that Goffy didn't know. The whisky was a mixture of whisky, brandy, and rum in equal parts.

A mile farther on, as he passed a house, a man named Arthur Watkins rushed out, yelling:

'Hey, where's Goffy?'

'Miles back,' Silas said. 'In a bad way. You ought to give give him a drink of summat when he comes by.'

Fifteen minutes later, when Goffy came by feeling as if he were running upstairs and his head knocking on the ceiling, Arthur Watkins rushed out with a tumbler of elderberry wine.

Goffy took hold of the elderberry wine and killed it one smack, and then went on with his eyes bulging out of his head like boss-marbles. He was mad with Silas and mad with himself. He couldn't see straight, and half a mile farther on a man rushed out of a row of cottages with a glass of parsnip wine eight years told. Goffy drank it in one blow and then rushed off again, feeling as if he were on a round-about.

'Hey! Not that way,' the man said. 'You're going back.'

By the time Goffy got as far as the bridge at Filmersham, and was lying down on the river bank, bathing his head in the water, my Uncle Silas was sitting in 'The Swan with Two Nicks' having a pint of draught ale with bread and cheese and a bunch of spring onions.

Everybody was very mad with Goffy, because the odds were extremely painful, and for many years Goffy was very mad with my Uncle Silas. Indeed, from that time onwards he never talked about races at all.

Races, on the other hand, appeared to interest my Uncle Silas more than ever.

'Goffy,' he would say, 'I know you ain't a reading man. But some day you ought to read about a race between the tortoise and the hare.'

THE DEATH OF UNCLE SILAS

THE DEATH OF UNCLE SILAS

WHEN I heard that my Great-uncle Silas was dying, I did not believe it. He was so old that it had always been hard for me to realize that he had ever been born. It had always seemed to me that he had simply turned up, very old and imperishable, with his crimson neckerchief and his bloodshot eye as bright as the neckerchief, his earth-coloured breeches, his winey breath, and that huskily devilish voice that had told me so many stories and had left as many tantalizingly half-told. Yet I remember how he would often tell me that he could recollect—the word was his own—standing on a corn-sheaf, in his frocks, and sucking at the breast his mother slipped out of her dress and held down for him in the harvest-field. 'They had the titty, them days, till they were damn near big enough to reap and tie.' Though he might very well have made it up. 'I was allus tidy thirsty,' he would say at the end of that story, or in fact at the end of any story. 'Mouthful o' wine?' he would say. It was his favourite phrase.

It was early autumn, in the middle of harvest, when I heard that he was dying. If it had been winter, or even spring, I might have believed it. But in autumn, and at harvest, it was unthinkable, absurd. His late peas would be coming into pod: for seventy years he had reckoned on them, without fail, for a last blow-out, with a goose and a dish of apple-sauce made from his own first cookers, on Michaelmas

Sunday. Who would pick the peas and gather the apples and lard the goose if he were to die? His potatoes would be dead ripe, the pears would be dropping into the golden orchard as mellow as honey, the elderberries would be drooping over the garden hedge in grape-dark bunches, ripe for wine. What would happen to them if Silas died? What could happen? No one else could dig those potatoes or garner those pears or work that wine as he did. The very words 'Silas is dying' seemed fantastic. Moreover I had heard them before. Hearing them once, I had hurried over to see him for the last time, only to find him up a ladder, pruning his apple trees with a jack-knife, all of a muck-sweat, with his jacket off, in the winter wind. 'I heard you were dead,' I said. He hawked and spat with a sort of gay ferocity. 'Ever hear the tale of the old gal who heard I was dead and buried, and then *seed* me in "The Swan"? She never touched another drop.'

When the news again came that he was dying I thought of his words. And I did not trouble to go over to see him. In imagination I saw him digging his potatoes in the hot September sun or mowing the half-acre of wheat he grew every other year at the end of the paddock, 'just so as I shan't forget how to swing a scythe.' The wheat kept him in bread, which he baked himself. He sent me a loaf sometimes, its crust as crisp as a wheat-husk and a dark earth-colour, and I often went over to help him band and carry the wheat. Even when I heard he was dying I expected every day to hear he had mown the wheat and was ready for me. I took as little notice of the news as that.

THE DEATH OF UNCLE SILAS

But unexpectedly there came other news:

'They say Silas doesn't know what he's doing half the time.'

Not 'Silas is ill,' or 'Silas is dying' or even 'Silas is unconscious,' but 'Silas doesn't know what he's doing.' The words were ominous, a contradiction of my Uncle Silas's whole life, his principles, his character, his amazing cunning, his devilish vitality. They perturbed me, for they could mean so much. They might mean that my Uncle Silas had so changed that he now no longer knew beer from water or wheat from beans; that he had dug his potatoes under-ripe or carried his wheat wet or made his wine from green elderberries. If it meant these things then it also meant the end. For what separated my Uncle Silas from other men was exactly this. He knew what he was doing. How often had I heard him say with a cock of his bloodshot eye and the most devilish darkness: 'I know what I'm doing, me boyo. I know what I'm doing.'

The day after hearing the news I went over to see him. His little stone reed-thatched house, squatting close under the shelter of the spinney of pines, was visible from afar off. There was always a puff of wood-smoke rising from the chimney, very blue against the black pines, winter and summer alike, if my Uncle Silas were at home. It was lovely September weather, the air breathless, the sunshine very soft and the pale amber colour of new wheat straw, and I saw the smoke rising up as straight as the pines themselves as I walked up the lane to the house.

It was a good sign. If the smoke were rising my Uncle

Silas was at home; if he were at home it was a thousand to one, in summer-time, that he was in the paddock or the garden, or if not there, by his chair at the window, his mole-coloured head and his scarlet neckerchief just visible among the very old, sweet-leaved white and mauve geraniums.

But that afternoon he was not in the paddock, where the wheat stood ripe and half-mown, and I could not see him in the garden, where the pears lay wasp-sucked and rotting in the yellowing grass. Walking up the garden-path, with the rank marigolds and untidy chrysanthemum stalks swishing heavily against my legs, I frightened a jay off the pea-rows. I stopped at once. But my Uncle Silas did not appear. The jay squawked in the wood. A jay on the pea-rows, and no sign from my Uncle Silas! I did not even look for him at the window, among the geraniums.

As I reached the door of the house I heard the clopping of the housekeeper's untied shoes coming along the stone passages to meet me. Before she appeared, I stepped over the threshold and looked into the room. The house was the same as ever, with the same eternal smell of earth and tea, of wood-smoke and balm, of geranium-leaves and wine. There was even the faint earth-smell of my Uncle Silas himself. But his chair was empty.

The housekeeper appeared a moment later, as scrawny and frigid as ever, and more straight-lipped, in the same black skirt and grey shirt-blouse and iron corsets that she seemed to have worn ever since my Uncle Silas had first engaged her, bringing with her as she had done for so many years, that smell of carbolic soap which had so often made him say, 'I do believe you were suckled on soap.' But that afternoon she looked tired, she seemed relieved to see me, and she broke out at once:

'Oh! dear, he'll wear me out.'

There was a sort of melancholy affection for him in her voice, and I knew at once that there must be something wrong.

'Where is he?' I asked.

But before she could reply his own cracked voice called suddenly:

'I'm here, me boyo, in here.'

'Where's that?' I called.

'In the parlour,' the housekeeper whispered.

'All among the fol-di-dols,' called my Uncle Silas. 'Come in.'

As I walked across the passage between the two rooms the housekeeper entreated me in another whisper, 'The doctor says you mustn't tire him.'

The doctor! My Uncle Silas not to be tired! He who could have mown a forty-acre field and not be tired! It was all over, I thought, as I pushed open the parlour-door and went in and met the stale antimacassar odour of the closed room.

And there, under the window, on an old black couch of American leather, with a green horse-rug over him and his sun-brown arms lying uselessly over the rug, lay my Uncle Silas. By his side was the night commode, and a little bamboo table with two wine-glasses and two bottles of lemon-coloured and blackish medicine on it.

'Now don't go and talk and tire yourself,' said the house-keeper.

'Go and wring yourself out, y'old wet sheet!' he croaked.

'What's that? If you ain't careful, I'll pack me bag and leave you lying there. So I'll tell you!'

'Pack it! And good riddance.'

'Ah, and I will!' She flashed off to the door.

It was the old game: she was always leaving and never leaving; my Uncle Silas was always dismissing her and always keeping her.

'Look slippy and bring us a bottle o' cowslip,' he said. 'And don't talk so much.'

But she was outside the door, without a word and not heeding him, before he had finished speaking. He lay back on the sofa, gloomily. 'Won't even let me wet me whistle,' he said.

He lay silent for a moment or two, his eyes watery, his chest heaving a little. 'I puff like an old frog,' he said. I did not answer, and until he regained his breath and his calmness I could not look at him again, and I let my eyes wander over the room instead, over the fol-di-dols he hated so much, the accumulated knick-knacks of nearly a hundred years, the little milky glass vases, rose-painted cups, mahogany tea-caddies, ruby wine-glasses, all the dear pretty things that he despised and never used. To find him there among them was a tragedy itself. He loved living things; and the only living things in that room were ourselves and the afternoon sunlight yellowing the closed window.

'Sit down,' he said at last. His voice so weary that I hardly

recognized it. 'Can you find a seat? All the damn chairs in this room are bum-slippy!'

I sat down on one of the black American leather chairs that matched his couch.

'Well,' I said. 'What's the matter with you?'

He shook his head. 'I ain't worth a hatful o' crabs.'

I could hardly bear the words. To hear that he didn't know what he was doing, to see a jay on his pea-rows, to find that he mustn't drink or talk or tire himself and now to hear him say, 'I ain't worth a hatful o' crabs.' My heart sank. It seemed to mean that his spirit was already dead. And no sooner had I thought it than he half-cocked his eye at me with a faint flicker of the old cunning.

'See that jay on the pea-rows?' he said.

'Yes.'

'Ah. I'll jay him.'

And then, with a sudden satanic flash of his bloodshot eye that surprised and delighted me, he whispered:

'Mouthful o' wine?'

I sat astonished. 'I thought they wouldn't let you drink?' I said.

He winked. 'In the medicine bottles,' he said. 'Elderberry in the dark and cowslip in the light. Pour out. Mouthful o' cowslip for me.'

Smiling, I poured out the wine and he lay smiling back at me with all his old subtlety and wickedness. As I gave him the glass he whispered: 'I fill 'em o' nights when she's a-bed.'

We drank in silence.

'What's the doctor say?' I asked.

'Says another drop o' wine will kill me.'

He finished his wine and wiped out the glass on the horse-blanket before putting it back on the table. The wine twinkled in his eyes and had already flushed away the dead yellow colour of his skin. And suddenly he shot up in bed, craning his tough thick neck to look out of the window:

'That jay again! God damn it, go and get my gun.'

I knew he meant it and I rose at once and went to the door. But he had raised his voice, and the housekeeper had heard him. She was in the room almost before I had moved, with the old despairing cry:

'Oh! he'll wear me out!'

She seized him sternly, forcing him back on the pillows while he shouted at her:

'You interferin' old tit! I'll shoot that jay if I have to shoot you first!'

'He don't know what he's saying or doin',' she said to me. And then to him, as she straightened his blankets inexorably:

'You'll take your medicine now, jay or no jay, and then get some sleep.'

As she took up the dark medicine bottle and poured out his measure into the wine-glass he kept lolling out his tongue, sick-fashion, and rolling his eyes and complaining, 'It's like drinking harness oil and vinegar, oh! it's like drinking harness oil and vinegar. Ach!'

'Drink it!' She forced the glass into his hands and he crooked his elbow on the pillow, lolling his tongue in and out.

She turned away to draw down the blinds. No sooner was her back turned than he lifted his glass and gave me a swift marvellous look of the wickedest triumph, licking his thick red lips and half-closing his bloodshot eye. The glass was empty and he was lying back on the pillows, smacking his mouth sourly, before she turned her head again.

'I'll come and see you,' I said, with my hand on the door-latch.

'Ah, do. I s'll have the taters out next week and the wheat down. Come and give us a hand.' The faint shadow of that wicked and triumphant smile flickered across his face. 'So long, me boyo.'

Outside, in the garden, I asked the housekeeper what was the matter with him.

'It's senile decay,' she said. 'He's losing the use of his legs and half the time he don't know what he's doing. It's just the medicine that keeps him going.' I had no doubt it was.

But one morning, a week later, I heard that he was dying; and in the afternoon I went over to the house. A gentle rain had been falling all morning, a quiet whispering September rain, and the air, very still and sultry, was saturated with the fragrance of wet pines. Crossing the paddock, I noticed that the wheat had been mown and half-banded and that the elderberries had gone from the garden-hedge. In the garden itself there was an intense rain-heavy stillness, unbroken except for the fretful twitter of swallows gathering on the house thatch. Looking across the rank thicket of dahlias and sunflowers beyond the apple trees I caught a glimpse of a dead blue jay strung on a hazel-stick among the pea-rows, its bright feathers dimmed with rain.

The housekeeper came to meet me at the door, her finger uplifted and her lips pursed tight to silence me.

'How is it with him?' I whispered.

'Bad,' she said. 'Very bad. He won't see to-morrow.'

'Can I see him?'

'He won't know you. He's very strange.'

Yes, he was very strange. He had begun to turn day into night, she told me: he would doze all day and then, in the dead of night, while she was asleep, he would wake and ferret in the cellar or mow his wheat and dig his potatoes and gather his elderberries for wine. She had suspected nothing until, awakened early one morning by a gun-shot, she had hurried into the garden to find him stringing up a dead jay in his pea-rows. It seemed that sometimes, too, he would drink his medicine in one swig, by the bottleful. He was so far gone as that.

When she had finished speaking I went into the house to look at him: he lay there, as before, on the leather couch, among the fol-di-dols, the green horse-rug over him and his brown hands lying listlessly outside it. He seemed to be asleep: yet there was something half-alert about the expression of his closed eyes, as though he were listening to me or perhaps to the rain. I stood for a moment watching him. And suddenly his eyes half-opened and a gaze that had in it some of the old strength and wickedness rested on me darkly. In a moment his lips moved too.

'What's the weather?' he said.

'It rains,' I said.

'Let it,' he whispered.

It was a flash of the old spirit. In a moment it was gone and his lips closed without another sound, and his eyelids lowered with a sharp flicker that was like a last wink at me.

I never heard him speak again. When we went in to him again, in the evening, he had turned day into night for the last time. The rain had ceased. The sun had broken through and was shining on the empty medicine bottles and his dead hands.

THE RETURN

THE RETURN

A LITTLE more than a year after my Uncle Silas died and was laid under the sycamores in the churchyard overlooking the river, I walked through the fields one afternoon to look for the last time at the little house by the pine spinney where he had lived for seventy years. It was soft autumn weather; the sunlight as mellow and still as Silas's cowslip wine.

As I went up the lane to the house I looked for the old sign of things: smoke rising from the chimney; the old summer bird-scares, age-green hats on sticks and inside-out umbrellas and twirling shuttlecocks; scarecrows made up of odd legs of Silas's pants and bell-bottomed trousers and the housekeeper's ancient hat and chemises; the ladder in the late apple trees; the bonfire filling the garden and the spinney and the fields with smoke that hung in sweet-smelling clouds under the pines and the golden cherry leaves. I listened for the cluck of Silas's hens and the grunting and rooting of the solitary sow he had always kept in the black sty under the elderberries at the garden end.

But it was very quiet, oddly silent everywhere. I could hear nothing. And then, coming to the garden gate, I saw that the gate and the fence, rain-green and patterned with prints of orange fungus for as long as I could remember, had been neatly repaired and painted white. The effect was curiously

sepulchral. But it did not trouble me. It was only when I saw, beyond the fence, the stump of a sawn-down apple tree, and then another, and then another of a cherry tree, and beyond that a wide empty space where the gooseberry trees had been, and beyond that another white fence in place of the old wild elderberry hedge, that I began to grow perturbed and finally angry. And for some minutes I stood there on the grass outside, helpless, staring at the white fences, the empty garden, the sawn-off tree-trunks, the newly white-painted windows until suddenly I could bear it no longer. It was the trees which finished me: lovely summer apple trees and the black-heart cherry trees and the yellow plums. Sawn down! Scrapped! God Almighty!

I opened the gate and slammed it shut again and walked up the path to the front door. It was shut—and painted white! The saintly effect of that repeated whiteness was too much. I hammered the door with my stick. I was pretty well worked up, ready for anything, with enough scorching irony ready on my lips to have burnt the paint off that door.

And then, waiting there, furious, I saw something else. The old sweet pink-and-white double roses that had grown on either side of the door for countless years had been sawn down too. The anger went out of me at once. I went listless. And there I stood; feeling pretty idiotic and as dumb as a brick, the irony evaporated with the anger, my whole spirit flat.

Then the door opened. And instantly my anger rose up again; but not bitterly. It was a sweet, nice anger—precise, juicy. My mouth was watering as though after a sour-sweet apple.

A young woman had opened the door. She too was dressed in white. She seemed to me like a paling out of the white fence; straight up and straight down, straight and white whichever way I looked at her. Her face was white, too: a pasty, town white. She was knitting. She carried the white wool and the white bone needles in her hands. She looked newly married. And, seeing me standing there, angry-faced, with the stick, she looked frightened.

'Good afternoon,' I said. I spoke nicely, sweetly, as though I wanted to sell her an insurance policy or a sewing machine.

'Good afternoon.' Her voice was prim: a white blameless-life kind of voice, decently distant, half afraid.

'I was wondering,' I said, 'if you would allow me to take some notes about the house and garden. They have—historic associations.'

She looked more scared than ever. I could see at once that she thought I was a liar and a trickster. Her white-knuckled hand was tight on the door, ready to slam it in my face. Her prim eyes were full of the fear that I was about to burst in and take the spoons and seduce her and help myself to the food in the pantry.

Then I said: 'I am a reporter. I represent *The Nenweald Telegraph*.'

The change in her was wonderful. She softened at once. She put the white knitting in the pocket of her white overall. But still a little of her fear remained.

'My husband isn't in,' she said.

'I have three children,' I told her.

The remark finished it all. For one moment she seemed to waver, in doubt, and then I said:

'It would make a nice little article. We might want a picture to go with it.'

I was saved again. She could see herself in the paper; the highest of all honours.

'I'm afraid I can't tell you much,' she said. 'We have only just come to live here. We are only just married.'

'Just so.'

I took out an old envelope and scribbled on it: 'White bridal veil.'

'When did you first occupy the house, Mrs.———?'

'Mrs. Wade-Brown. Early this summer.'

'Who lived here before that?'

'An awful old man. I didn't know him, but the place was in an awful state. Seeds hung up in paper bags all over the bedroom ceilings. Rotten apples on the bedroom floors. And there was no bathroom. We had to have a bathroom put in.'

'You had to have a bathroom put in,' I said, and I wrote on the envelope: 'White bath.'

'He was a terrible old man who lived here,' she said.

'I know,' I said.

'Did you know him?' she said.

'Everybody knew him. He was famous—notorious.'

'We found hundreds of empty bottles in the cellar,' she said. 'He must have done nothing else but drink.'

'He didn't,' I said. 'He drank himself to death.'

She was speechless.

'It was the cellar I wanted to see,' I said. 'It is the cellar which is historic.'

She hesitated.

'In what way historic?' she asked. 'I was a school-teacher before I was married. I never heard of it.'

'A man hid there,' I said. 'A sort of conspirator. A long time ago.' I was not lying now: it was true. My Great-uncle Silas had hidden there, with the police of half the county looking for him, though that is another story.

I began to wipe my boots on the doormat, scribbling with mock deference on the old envelope all the time.

And, finally, she led me into the house. Stepping over the threshold, I breathed in at once, instinctively, to catch the smells of old tea and earth and wine and geraniums, all the warm rich odours of my Uncle Silas's long existence there. But the air was dead: stale with the odours of new French-polished furniture and wool rugs and oilcloth. And one look at the room was enough: the prim, black-framed verses on the clear walls, new fire-grate in place of the old faggot-oven, the wedding presents all arranged on the piano and the side-board with the correctitude of a showroom in a furniture shop. There was something ice-cold about its parsimonious respectability.

The woman saw me looking at it. 'It's very different from when we found it,' she said.

'Very different.'

'You must mind the stairs down to the cellar. They're very dark. We never use it.'

'Perhaps I'd better go first,' I said. 'I could light a match for you.'

'No, no. I'll get a candle.'

There was a spirit of devilry in me, a sudden inheritance from my Uncle Silas himself, and suddenly, while she was looking for the candle in the back-kitchen, I slipped down the stairs as quickly and easily as unbuttoning the button of an old waistcoat—zip!

Then at the bottom, turning and looking up again, I saw the woman's face above the unlighted candle. She looked scared again.

'What happened?' she said. 'Did you fall? Wait a minute. I'll bring the candle.'

She came timidly down the dark stairs, and I took the candle at the bottom and struck a match and lighted it.

We were in the cellar. And suddenly I breathed. It was like the breath of another world: the wine and dampness, the musty odour of ferment and dust and spider-webs. The walls were yellow in the candle-light. Big shadows fell and ballooned over them as I raised and lowered the candle.

'Was it in here he hid?' she said.

'In here.'

And then I saw something: bottles, dark, dust-covered bottles, six or seven of them, standing in the darkest corner.

'Bottles,' I said. I tried to be casual, indifferent, as though bottles could mean nothing to me.

'Where?' she said. 'I thought the cellar was empty.'

I put the candle on the stone floor and took up one of the bottles. It was full. I held it in my hand for a moment in

suspense. Then I took out the cork and sniffed. It was wine, elderberry. I did not know what to do with myself. I was smelling the wine again when the woman said:

'What is it?'

'Vinegar,' I said. 'Smell.'

She smelled. 'It's a queer vinegar,' she said.

'It's worked,' I said, 'fermented. It's in a state of ferment.'

I hardly knew what I was saying. I put back the cork and picked up another bottle and uncorked that and sniffed again. It was elderberry.

'Vinegar,' I said.

Then I took up another bottle and another and another.

'They're all vinegar,' I said.

Then suddenly I saw a bottle of light glass: I could see the wine in the candlelight, glowing with the lovely translucent cowslip light I knew so well.

'What's that?' she said.

I smelled. The old delicate flower aroma of the wine was wonderful.

'Harness oil,' I said.

I put the cork back before she could move or speak. There were still two other bottles. I picked them up and sniffed of them and recorked them before she could wink.

'All harness oil,' I said.

'The old man left them. That awful old man,' she said.

But I was looking at the bottles in mock perplexity.

'They're dangerous,' I said.

'How? Dangerous!'

'They may burst—blow up. You'd better get rid of them.'

I picked up the candle. 'Get a sack and we'll put them in and I'll dump them in the ditch when I go.'

'Would you?'

Five minutes later we came up the cellar steps again, she carrying the candle, I with the sack of wine on my back.

'Outside,' she kept saying. 'Outside. Whatever you do, put them outside.'

I laid the sack tenderly on the earth outside the door.

'It's very good of you,' she said. 'Have you taken all the notes you want?'

'I should like to see the garden,' I said.

We walked together down the garden path. The place had been ruined: a neat, parsimonious little lawn had been laid down where Silas had grown his potatoes; the old sunflowers had gone and the old lilac trees; the place where the loveliest of all lilies had grown was a bed of red geraniums. I could not bear it. Only the thought of the sackful of harness oil and vinegar kept me from flying into anger again.

Then, at the foot of the garden, I saw something which almost shocked me. It was the pig-sty. The lilacs and cherry trees and lilies and roses had gone, but the pig-sty remained.

'You keep pigs?' I said.

'Oh, no, no. I should be sick.'

'But there's the sty.'

'Oh, but it's empty. It's going to be knocked down. My husband is going to knock it down. We shall use it for firewood when winter comes.'

I leaned over the sty-rails and looked on dung-stained

bricks and whitewashed shelter. Then I unlatched the gate and walked into the sty. I was just bending down to look through the pig-door when the woman cried out:

'Oh, don't go in there!'

'I'm very sorry,' I said.

'There's a gun in there.'

'A gun?'

'It's been there ever since we came. My husband found it. It's loaded. He daren't let it off.'

I looked at her seriously.

'Have you a licence?'

'Oh, no.'

'You know you can get into serious trouble for having a gun without a licence,' I said.

'Trouble? No!'

'Yes,' I said. 'And then guns are dangerous. You say it's loaded?'

'Yes.' She was scared, whiter than ever.

'I'd better have a look at it,' I said.

I bent down and went into the inner sty. The floor was still strawed and the gun was hanging on a nail on the wooden wall. I took it down. It was plainly my Uncle Silas's gun. His name was lettered on the stock in crude letters almost smoothed out again by use and time. It was an old muzzle-loader, and the barrel had been stuffed with paper and filings and old nails and ball bullets and powder. I had seen my Uncle Silas knocked flat on his back into the potatoes with the kick of it.

After a moment I went through into the sty-yard, carrying

the gun in my hand as carelessly as though it had been a banana.

The woman retreated away.

'Do be careful,' she said.

'All right,' I said. 'I'm going to let it off.'

She was terrified. 'When? How?'

'Have you got some string?' I said. 'Good string. A long piece.'

She fled into the house. While she was gone I leaned the gun against the sty-rail and stared about the garden, trying hard to find some object in it that I could blow to smithereens, but the place was as bare as a piece of ploughedland. And very soon the woman came running back with the string in her hands.

'You won't hurt anything? You'll be careful? You won't do any damage?'

I began to fix the gun to the sty-rails, lashing it with string, and when that was finished I tied the remaining string to the trigger.

The woman was trembling.

'You're not frightened?' I said. I spoke sweetly to her, with the greatest consideration.

She shook her head.

'You must stand away,' I said.

At first she stood a yard or two away, and then ten yards, and then when she saw me cocking the gun and letting out the string she was thirty yards off, and the last I saw of her was as she stood on the threshold of the house, with her hands over her ears and her face as white as her wool.

A second later I pulled the string. The bang was terrific, shattering. I had aimed the gun at the pines, and the moment after the shot had torn through the trees there was a sound as though the sky were suddenly hailing cotton reels. And then before the last of the pine-cones had clattered down it seemed as though I had peppered all the rooks and jackdaws in the parish. There was nothing but a wild sound of the cawing and squalling birds flying high over the garden and the pines in the still, autumn air.

It was a wild, crazy sound, and it brought the woman running out of the house again.

'Is it all right? What have you done? What is it?'

I was untying the gun from the sty-rails as she came up, and I turned to her and spoke with great seriousness again.

'You see what might have happened,' I said. 'You see? This gun is so old it might have burst.'

She nodded.

'I'll take the gun away and ditch it with the bottles,' I said. 'It's no good.'

The rooks were still flying wildly round and round, and the sound of their calling and of my voice seemed to terrify her into acquiescence. She said nothing, and I finished untying the gun.

We walked back up the path in silence, the rooks and daws still circling madly above the pines. It was not until we reached the house that she spoke at all.

'I'm sorry you had that trouble,' she said. She spoke as if I had done her a great service. 'I shall be glad to be rid of the awful things.'

'I'm sure you will.'

'My husband is a teetotaller, and he doesn't shoot,' she paused. 'Have you got your notes?'

'I've got my notes,' I said.

We stood in silence for a moment, awkwardly. I wanted to get away before her suspicions began again and she sent for the police, and I began to screw up the neck of the sack in readiness to swing it over my shoulder.

And then she remembered something.

'Once before,' she said, 'someone else came and wanted to look round the house.'

'Yes?'

'A woman,' she said. 'She said she wanted to look at the place again for the last time.'

For some reason I could find nothing to say, and I stood in silence while she told me of how on a day in summer a woman—it could only have been my Uncle Silas's housekeeper—walked into the garden and stood there like someone stupefied, not saying much except to repeat at intervals that she wanted the old bath. 'I should like the old bath as a keepsake, to do my washing in.' The young woman didn't understand her, and then the old woman stood there in the garden and began to cry, still saying that she wanted the old bath, until finally, as the young woman herself said to me, 'I had to send her away because I could see she was either drunk or wrong in the head.'

I picked up the sack and slung it on my shoulder. 'I shan't want to carry it far,' I said.

'It's good of you to carry it at all,' she said.

A moment later I thanked her and said good afternoon and opened the white garden gate and began to walk down the lane with the sack filled with the bottles on my shoulder.

At the foot of the lane I turned back. She was still standing there, at the white gate, watching me, as though she were still thinking about me.

I was thinking, too. But not of her, or the changed house, or the desolated garden, or the heavy wine-bottles clanking in the sack, or even my Uncle Silas himself.

I was thinking instead of that tart and irascible house-keeper, a flint-hearted iron-corseted woman, a tartar, a sour old tyrant, standing there in the summer garden, all broken up and stupefied, weeping her heart out for something nobody would ever understand.

FULL COLOUR
CAPTAIN UNDERPANTS
AND THE Tyrannical Retaliation OF THE TURBO TOILET 2000

The Eleventh Epic Novel by
DAV PILKEY

with colour by Jose Garibaldi
and Corey Barba

SCHOLASTIC

Published in the UK by Scholastic, 2022
Euston House, 24 Eversholt Street, London, NW1 1DB
Scholastic Ireland, 89E Lagan Road,
Dublin Industrial Estate, Glasnevin, Dublin, D11 HP5F

First published in the US by Scholastic Inc., 2014

Text and illustrations © Dav Pilkey, 2014

ISBN 978 0702 31287 8

A CIP catalogue record for this book is available from the British Library.

Printed by C&C, China

1 3 5 7 9 10 8 6 4 2

www.scholastic.co.uk

Cover design by Dav Pilkey and Phil Falco
Book design by Dav Pilkey, Kathleen Westray and Phil Falco
Colour by Jose Garibaldi and Corey Barba
Colour flatting by Amanda Barba

FULL COLOUR

CAPTAIN UNDERPANTS

AND THE TYRANNICAL RETALIATION OF THE TURBO TOILET 2000

The Eleventh Epic Novel by

DAV PILKEY

with colour by Jose Garibaldi and Corey Barba

SCHOLASTIC

CHAPTERS

the truth, the whole truth, and nothing but the truth about CAPTAIN UNDERPants

Once There was Two supa-awesome Kids named George and Harold.

We rock Da house, son!

me Too!

But they had a mean Prinsiple named Mr. Krupp.

BLah-Biddy BLah BLah BLah!

Mr. Krupp Tried To BLackmale George and Harold.

I GOT You now!

VIDeo EvideNse

So George and Harold Hipnitized him.

I don't think so!!!

They made him think He was captain underpants!

Captain Underpants

it was funny at First...

But then He took things a little too far!

Tra-La-Laaaa!

Hey come Back!

He got into all sorts of ~~trouble~~ Troubel.

Then one day he drank some alien super power Juice...

...and he got REAL super powers.

Wich got him into even MORE TrouBeL.

Now, whenever Mr. Krupp Hears somebody snap thier Fingers...

SNAP

...He Turns into Captain Underpants.

Tra-La Laaaa!

and whenever anybody pours water on CAPTain underpantses head...

He turns Back into mean old Mr. Krupp.

BLaH BLah BLah

One time the TALKinG ToiLeTs atacked.

Yum Yum

eat em up!

There Leader was The Turbo ToiLet 2000.

George and Harold used a wierd mashine To make a good Robot called the RoBo PLunGer.

Patsy 2000

the robo Plunger
Beated up the
Turbo Toilet 2000

and Flew him
To uranus.

welcome to uranus

THere they
have stayed For
many months.

This other time,
wedgie woman
made 2 robots.

one of them Kicked
a kickball into
outer space.

could these
two events
Be ~~connected~~
connected ?

Our heros are about to find out!

Because at this very mo-mint...

they are treveling backwerds in time to discover the terrible truth!

OH NO!

Here we GO agaivh!

© Tree House comix

CHAPTER 1
GEORGE AND HAROLD

This is George Beard and Harold Hutchins. George is the kid on the left with the tie and the flat-top. Harold is the one on the right with the T-shirt and the bad haircut. Remember that now.

If you're confused by what's going on here, don't worry. They're confused, too. You see, George, Harold, and Captain Underpants had just undergone an epic adventure that started out in the dinosaur age and ended at their school—thirty years in the future. Now, thanks to Melvin Sneedly (the tattletale genius) and his glow-in-the-dark, time-traveling Robo-Squid suit, they were all hurtling backward in time. Back a long, long, long time ago to that dull, old-fashioned age known as the present.

Oh, I almost forgot. Traveling with them were three purple-and-orange-speckled eggs, laid by their pet pterodactyl, Crackers, who, along with their other pet—Sulu the Bionic Hamster—had just saved the planet *and* created all life as we know it, simultaneously.

See? That wasn't confusing at all, was it?

Melvin's glow-in-the-dark, time-traveling Robo-Squid suit whizzed through time in a dazzling array of electrified eye candy as thirty years sped by in reverse.

Then everything stopped suddenly.
George and Harold looked around.

"Hey," said Harold. "We're still here
at school!"

"Correct," said Melvin. "Only it's now
thirty years and one day earlier."

"Hey, look," said George, pointing at the school. "There's Tippy and his Robo-Pants."

"Not again," Harold moaned.

"Relax," said Melvin, as a flash of green light shot out of the library window. "You're looking at something that happened yesterday, remember?"

"Oh, yeah," said Harold. "We were up there in the library. We just disappeared in the Purple Potty!"

"Right," said George. "And Tippy is just about to come after us. He should be leaving any second now."

Suddenly, a crackling blue light shot out of the Robo-Pants, and before you could say "convoluted plotline," it disappeared into the noontime haze.

"OK," said Melvin. "Here you are. Home again, home again, jiggity jig! Take your precious eggs and go about your business!"

"Wait a second," said George. "Aren't the cops still after us?"

"Yeah," said Harold. "Don't they still think we stole that money from the bank?"

"Not anymore," said Melvin proudly, patting himself on the back with one of his mechanical tentacles. "Luckily, I had this glow-in-the-dark, time-traveling Robo-Squid suit in my garage. I used it to go back in time and hack into the bank's computer."

"What for?" asked Harold.

"No big deal," said Melvin. "I altered their surveillance images a little bit. Just don't grow a mustache or a beard anytime soon, and you guys'll be fine."

"Wow," said Harold. "Melvin Sneedly rescued us. I can't believe it!"

"Yeah, I don't get it, Melvin," said George suspiciously. "You've always hated us. How come you're being so nice to us all of a sudden?"

"Oh, I have my reasons," said Melvin. "I have my reasons."

And Melvin did indeed have reasons. One whole year's worth of reasons. But before I can tell you that story, I have to tell you *this* story . . .

CHAPTER 2
DON'T YOU HATE IT
WHEN A KICKBALL
HITS URANUS?

Somewhere in the deepest, darkest reaches
of our solar system, a red rubber kickball was
zooming through space. None of Earth's top
scientists could explain where it had come
from, or why it was racing toward Uranus,
but it had been on its present course for
the past five and a half books, and
nothing could stop it.

The kickball sped closer and closer to a small cluster of porcelain monstrosities that lay together in a heap on the surface of the icy, ridiculously named planet. Behind them, guarding them all with a keen, observant eye, was a robotic sentinel known as the Incredible Robo-Plunger. Faster and faster the kickball whizzed toward them, until finally . . .

The force of the red rubber ball knocked the head right off of the Incredible Robo-Plunger. The decapitated defender jutted forward slightly, as Photo-Atomic Trans-Somgobulating Yectofantriplutoniczanziptomistic juice drizzled out from its mangled neck hole and oozed slowly downward into the gaping mouth of the Turbo Toilet 2000.

This was unfortunate, because as any robotics engineer will tell you, it's very important to keep Photo-Atomic Trans-Somgobulating Yectofantriplutoniczanziptomistic juice as far away from evil robots as possible.

You certainly don't want to get even a drop of it in their mouths, for it will only make them come to life and give them an unquenchable appetite for destruction. Which, sadly, is exactly what happened that bleak night on the terribly gassy surface of Uranus.

The Turbo Toilet 2000's bulbous, bloodshot eyes smacked open and wobbled around wildly. His massive left arm creaked up and rubbed the painful, throbbing side of his porcelain lid.

"Where the heck am I?" he said, looking around at his fallen allies. Clumsily, he squeaked to his feet, dusted himself off, and beheld the headless mess that once was the Incredible Robo-Plunger. Then it all came back to him. The battle. The defeat. The humiliation.

It wasn't long before the Turbo Toilet 2000 had pieced together every single event that had brought him and his army of Talking Toilets to this frozen, frustrating fate.

"I must retaliate," he said, clenching his razor-sharp porcelain teeth together tightly. "I must avenge my fallen allies!"

Luckily for him, he was a robot, which meant that he knew a thing or two about mechanical engineering. It didn't take long for him to disassemble the Robo-Plunger, rearrange the pieces, and create a flying rocket scooter from the recycled parts of his arch-enemy.

The only thing left to do was to travel the
long journey from Uranus to Earth. It was a
voyage that would take him nearly three whole
pages to complete. And when he arrived, he
would wage a war against the good people
of Earth. A war that would threaten the very
foundation of our planet. But before I can tell
you that story, I have to tell you *this* story . . .

CHAPTER 3
MELVIN'S MOMENT
OF MIRTH

Remember back in chapter 1 where we found out that Melvin had a whole year's worth of reasons why he needed to bring George and Harold and Captain Underpants back to the present? Well, in case you're wondering what happened during that year, here's what happened during that year:

Immediately after our heroes disappeared on their prehistoric journey, the cops started looking for George, Harold, and Mr. Krupp. Wanted posters appeared in post offices across America. But, since George and Harold and Mr. Krupp had traveled back in time to the Cretaceous period, they were nowhere to be found.

WANTED

FOR BANK ROBBERY

Everyone assumed that George, Harold, and Mr. Krupp had robbed a bank and were hiding out in Canada or Mexico somewhere, and it wasn't too long before the cops gave up and stopped looking for them.

This was sad news for most of the residents of Piqua, Ohio, but not for Melvin Sneedly. Melvin was finally happy for the first time in years. No George and no Harold meant no pranks, no comics, and, best of all, no interruptions. Melvin could finally go about conducting his scientific experiments, creating wild new inventions, and indulging his beautiful mind in peace.

But all that happiness only lasted for about two weeks, because, as we mentioned earlier . . .

. . . *you-know-who* showed up.

CHAPTER 4
HE-WHO-MUST-NOT-
BE-FLUSHED

The Turbo Toilet 2000 entered Earth's
atmosphere in a blazing fireball from the sky.
His rocket scooter roared over the rooftops of
the small Ohio town as the porcelain predator
bellowed out an eardrum-crushing taunt,
"HEEEEEEEEERE'S JOHNNY!"

Then came the destruction. Buildings collapsed. City buses were thrown through skyscraper windows. Fires raged out of control. The chaos and devastation crippled the town, sent residents running for their lives . . . and annoyed the heck out of one little boy.

Melvin Sneedly had been trying to get
some work done in his bedroom laboratory
when the attack began. All he needed was
one or two more hours of uninterrupted
silence to complete his experiment, but the
terrible ruckus outside was really getting
on his nerves. Melvin marched over to his
bedroom window, poked his head out, and
shouted, "HEY! I'm trying to *WORK*, you
idiot! BE *QUIET*!!!"

As you can probably imagine, the Turbo Toilet 2000 didn't take too kindly to being dressed down in such a manner. He swiveled his massive bowl around quickly and glared at Melvin with raging, hard-boiled eyeballs.

"Uh-oh," Melvin gulped.

Suddenly, the Turbo Toilet 2000 leaped at Melvin. The tiny tattletale screamed as the malevolent miscreant chased him down the street, across the city, and into the empty, darkened hallways of Jerome Horwitz Elementary School.

Melvin ran upstairs and hid under Mr. Krupp's desk while the Turbo Toilet 2000 searched through the classrooms for him. Melvin was in deep trouble. Finally, he *actually* needed Captain Underpants's help, but the Waistband Warrior was nowhere to be found.

"Rats!" said Melvin. "If only I could— *OUCH*!" Melvin's knee was pressing down into something sharp. Carefully, Melvin reached down and pulled the pointy little object out of his knee.

It was a toenail.

Not just any toenail, either. It was one of Mr. Krupp's thick, greasy, yellow toenails that he had clipped off the day before he had been whisked away on his journey back through time.

"Ewwww! What a slob!" said Melvin, as he flicked the toenail away. Then Melvin thought of something. He knew that Mr. Krupp was also Captain Underpants. That meant that Mr. Krupp's DNA must have some kind of super-powered element in its makeup. If Melvin could find a way to extract the super-powered element from Mr. Krupp's DNA, Melvin could, theoretically, transfer those super powers to himself!

"Where's that toenail?" cried Melvin.

CHAPTER 5
BIG MELVIN RETURNS

The Turbo Toilet 2000 noisily smashed his way from classroom to classroom, getting closer to Mr. Krupp's office with each thundering footstomp. Melvin desperately searched the mangy, orange carpet for Mr. Krupp's stinky toenail, digging his fingers deep into the matted shag as the sounds of carnage got louder and louder.

"Where's that toenail?" Melvin screamed.

Finally, Mr. Krupp's office door burst open.

"A-HA!" shouted the Turbo Toilet 2000.
"I'VE GOT YOU NOW, YOU ANNOYING
LITTLE BRAT!" He reached down, grabbed
Melvin by the foot, and pulled him toward
his chomping, razor-sharp teeth.

"NOOOOOO," screamed Melvin. "I'M TOO
GIFTED TO DIE! I'M TOO TALENTED! I'M
TOO—*OUCH*!"

Once again, Mr. Krupp's stinky toenail had lodged its way into Melvin's pasty, freckled skin. But this time, Melvin couldn't have been happier about it. Quickly, he reached back, untied his shoe, and slipped his foot out. Then Melvin jumped out of Mr. Krupp's window and slid down the flagpole, with the Turbo Toilet 2000 in hot pursuit.

Fortunately, Melvin's Li'l Scientist Wristwatch had a built-in DNA extractor. Melvin inserted the filthy toenail into his watch and programmed a complete extraction procedure while the Turbo Toilet 2000 chased him back through town.

As Melvin ran screaming, his watch quickly pulverized and sonicated the toenail cells, removed the membrane lipids, proteins, and RNA, and purified and isolated a single strand of Mr. Krupp's DNA.

When Melvin reached his bedroom laboratory, he quickly fed the results into his Mecha-Computer, which identified the metallo-organic, "super-powered" substance and began replicating it in a saline gel solution. The gel percolated slowly as it oozed into a glass beaker.

"Hurry up, you dumb semiconservative genome replication device!" shouted Melvin, as the Turbo Toilet 2000 crashed through his bedroom wall.

"Gotcha!" roared the loathsome lavatory.
He scooped Melvin into his gigantic fist as
his wet, leathery tongue slid back and forth
against his pointed porcelain premolars.

With one final, desperate thrust,
Melvin grabbed the beaker and
chugged down its green,
glowing contents.

The Turbo Toilet 2000 popped Melvin
into his mouth like a cocktail weenie and
started to chew. His ferocious fangs chomped
feverishly, but Melvin was tough and hard
and surprisingly gristly. Then the Turbo
Toilet 2000 struggled to swallow, a task that
he found nearly impossible.

With his gigantic metal fingers, he reached
into his bowl and pulled out a mucus-covered
little boy, who, surprisingly, didn't have a
scratch on him. The Turbo Toilet 2000 gawked
at Melvin in dumbfounded astonishment.

"You are _so_ immature," said Melvin.

CHAPTER 6
SANITIZED FOR
YOUR PROTECTION

Unfortunately, the epic fight that followed was WAY too violent and disturbing to appear in a children's book. The images and descriptions would just be too terrifying. You'd have nightmares for weeks, trust me!

So I have invited a guest illustrator, Timmy Swanson (age four), to draw the action in a style that won't depict too much graphic detail. I've also asked his nana, Gertrude (age seventy-one), to describe the scene in her own gentle vocabulary.

Take it away, Timmy and Nana!

Thank you, dear. Well, let's see what's
happening here. What – oh, my. That . . .
that's horrible!

It looks like a little boy is – oh,
dear. Now what's he doing? Oh, dear me!
This certainly is not appropriate
at all!

And now
there's a robot
shaped like a—well, I'd rather not
say. He's just doing such dreadful
things, though. And—OH! Oh, my.
Say, what kind of a book is this?
Oh, for heaven's sake! This is
ridiculous. I've never been so
offended in all my—OH! I've seen
just about enough—OH! OH!!! Oh, dear!

Timmy! Stop drawing! Stop drawing this instant!

No, Timmy! No!

CHAPTER 7
THE INCREDIBLY GRAPHIC VIOLENCE CHAPTER, PART 1 (IN FLIP-O-RAMA™)

PILKEY® BRAND
⊃·RAMA

HERE'S HOW IT WORKS!

STEP 1
First, place your *left* hand inside the dotted lines marked "LEFT HAND HERE." Hold the book open *flat*.

STEP 2
Grasp the *right-hand* page with your right thumb and index finger (inside the dotted lines marked "RIGHT THUMB HERE").

STEP 3
Now *quickly* flip the right-hand page back and forth until the picture appears to be *animated*.

(For extra fun, try adding your own sound-effects!)

FLIP-O-RAMA 1

(pages 53 and 55)

Remember, flip *only* page 53.
While you are flipping, be sure you
can see the picture on page 53
and the one on page 55.
If you flip quickly, the two
pictures will start to look like
<u>one</u> *animated* picture.

Don't forget to
add your own sound-effects!

LEFT HAND HERE

OH, DEAR!!!

RIGHT
THUMB
HERE

54

OH, DEAR!!!

FLIP-O-RAMA 2

(pages 57 and 59)

Remember, flip *only* page 57.
While you are flipping, be sure you
can see the picture on page 57
and the one on page 59.
If you flip quickly, the two
pictures will start to look like
<u>one</u> *animated* picture.

Don't forget to
add your own sound-effects!

LEFT HAND HERE

OH, MY!!!

RIGHT
THUMB
HERE

RIGHT
INDEX
FINGER
HERE

OH, MY!!!

FLIP-O-RAMA 3

(pages 61 and 63)

Remember, flip *only* page 61.
While you are flipping, be sure you
can see the picture on page 61
and the one on page 63.
If you flip quickly, the two
pictures will start to look like
<u>one</u> *animated* picture.

Don't forget to
add your own sound-effects!

LEFT HAND HERE

OH, FOR GOODNESS' SAKE!!!

RIGHT
THUMB
HERE

OH, FOR
GOODNESS' SAKE!!!

CHAPTER 8
EVERYBODY LOVES MELVIN

When it was all over, the Turbo Toilet 2000 was dead and Melvin Sneedly was a HERO! The mayor had a big parade in honor of Melvin. "Weird Al" Yankovic wrote a song about him. Even the vice president sent a letter of congratulations!

Melvin Sneedly was known throughout the world as the little, super-powered tattletale who saved the world.

"Finally!" said Melvin. "I'm getting the respect I deserve!"

CHAPTER 9
WITH GREAT POWER COMES A GREAT BIG PAIN IN THE HINEY

Melvin enjoyed being a superhero—at first. It was fun stopping runaway trains, rescuing lost children, and saving people from burning buildings. Whenever anybody needed help, all they had to do was lift their heads to the sky and cry out, "YO! Big Melvin!" And Big Melvin would drop whatever he was doing and zip to the scene and save the day. It was all good, at first . . . until it started to get bad.

You see, after a while people started to
abuse the system. They started crying out
"YO! Big Melvin!" all the time, and it got old
pretty quickly.

Melvin would drop everything, throw on
his cape, fly out the window, zip through the
city, and arrive at the scene, only to find out
that it wasn't an emergency at all. Usually
it was just someone who had misplaced her
cell phone . . . or a kid who needed help
with a video game cheat code . . . or some
guy who had accidentally dropped his
wallet in the toilet.

It was a complete waste of Melvin's time, and the interruptions were beginning to drive him crazy.

But the final straw came one evening as Melvin was doing a synchrotron radiation experiment with his homemade oscillating-field particle accelerator. Eleven months of research were finally about to pay off. The klystrons and electromagnets began to accelerate the hadrons faster and faster through Melvin's homemade copper cyclone tubing. Soon, Melvin would be the first person on Earth to definitively prove the Higgs boson's existence and solve the mystery of everything.

But then, with his supersonic eardrums, Melvin heard a cry for help from across the city.

Quickly, Melvin shut down his experiment, which caused the particle accelerator to overheat. The resulting explosion blew a hole in his bedroom floor forty feet deep. But Melvin didn't care. Somewhere in the city, a citizen needed his help. So he grabbed his smoldering cape from the pile of ashes that used to be his bedroom closet and flew to the scene of the emergency.

When he arrived, he found a middle-aged woman screaming frantically out her apartment window. "YO! Big Melvin! HELP!!! HELP!!! It's an emergency!!!"

"What's wrong?" Melvin asked desperately.

"Do these pants make me look fat?" asked
the lady.

CHAPTER 10
IT'S A MAD, MAD, MAD, MAD MELVIN

Melvin was angry. Very, very angry. Since he'd become a superhero, he'd had no time to do his experiments. He'd had no time off, no sleep, no privacy, no time for *anything*. At that moment, Melvin made a decision. He decided, for his own sanity, to quit the superhero business once and for all. But getting *out* was going to be a lot harder than it was getting in. Melvin needed to find a superhero to replace him. So he made up his mind to locate Captain Underpants, bring him back to Piqua, and let *him* deal with all the hassles of superherodom.

Finding Captain Underpants, it turns out, wasn't as hard as Melvin had expected. Melvin knew that George and Harold were usually with Captain Underpants, and Sulu the Bionic Hamster was usually with George and Harold.

"So," Melvin concluded, "if I find Sulu, I *should* find Captain Underpants!"

Since Melvin had installed a GPS on Sulu's robotic endoskeleton, all Melvin had to do was run a simple scan on his computer for the GPS device. At first, the scan found nothing. So Melvin broadened his search to include all locations *and all times*. Finally, Melvin's search paid off. He found Sulu's last satellite-reported location, down by the schoolyard, twenty-nine years in the future.

"That wasn't too hard," Melvin sneered. "But bringing them all back to the present will be a little more complicated!"

CHAPTER 11
DARK FORESHADOWS

Melvin went to his garage and climbed into his glow-in-the-dark, time-traveling Robo-Squid suit. Quickly, the suit powered up and started slinking and slithering toward the schoolyard as Melvin began the long journey to bring George, Harold, and Captain Underpants back home where they belonged.

After solving some surveillance photo issues at the bank, Melvin zapped himself to the future, fetched everyone, and brought them all back one year earlier to the exact time and place where they had departed on their journey in our last book.

George, Harold, and Captain Underpants had been through a lot in the past few days, but now it was as if they had never left at all. Everything was just as it had been.

The Turbo Toilet 2000 wouldn't arrive on Earth for another two weeks, so Melvin's future as a superhero would never become reality. And nobody was happier about that than Melvin himself.

"I don't have to be a superhero anymore!" cried Melvin happily. "I can finally follow my destiny! Peace and quiet at last!"

"But you still haven't told us why you've brought us back," said George.

"Yeah," said Harold. "What gives?"

"Oh, you'll find out," said Melvin with a foreboding chuckle. "In two weeks, you'll find out!" Melvin unleashed a horrible, villainous laugh as his glow-in-the-dark Robo-Squid suit began to shake and buzz. Soon, he and his tentacled time machine disappeared into a ball of electric light.

CHAPTER 12
HEADIN' HOME

George and Harold had no choice but to take Mr. Krupp home. They brought him to his front door, got the key out from behind the bushes, and let him inside.

"Go over to the kitchen sink and splash some water on your face," said George.

"Aye, aye, sir!" said Captain Underpants.

He did as he was told, and in no time at all he was back to his grumpy old self.

"I wonder what's going to happen in two weeks," said Harold, as he and George walked home.

"Aw, I'm sure it's no big deal," said George. "If Melvin can handle it, *WE* can handle it!"

Soon, George and Harold were back up
in their tree house. Carefully, they placed
Crackers's eggs on some soft pillows under a
few desk lamps.

"There," said George. "That should keep
them warm and cozy!"

George and Harold were dead tired. They
hadn't slept in over thirty hours, and they'd
been running for their lives most of that time.

"I need a *serious* nap," said Harold, as he settled into his beanbag chair.

"Me, too," said George, as he collapsed into his own beanbag chair. "Saving the world is exhausting!"

"I'm still a little worried about that whole 'two weeks' thing," said Harold. "That sounds really bad!"

"Relax," said George. "There's nothing we can do about it now, anyway."

"Let's try to stay out of trouble for the next two weeks," said Harold. "If the world is going to end, I don't want to be stuck in detention the whole time."

"Aw, don't worry so much," said George. "Besides, how much trouble could we get into in two weeks, anyway?"

CHAPTER 13
ELEVEN
MINUTES LATER

"GEORGE!"

"HAROLD!!!"

"GET DOWN HERE RIGHT NOW!!!"

George and Harold opened their eyes. Wearily, they stumbled to the tree house door and looked down. George's mom and dad and Harold's mom were all standing down in the yard looking very angry.

"The school called," George's dad said. "They told us that you kids weren't in class today!"

"Uh-oh," said George.

"We're dead," said Harold.

"Would you mind explaining what you've been doing all day?" asked Harold's mom angrily.

George and Harold could hide the truth no longer. They decided to confess everything.

"We couldn't go to school today," said George. "We had to save the Earth from an evil, crazy guy who was riding around in a giant pair of robotic pants."

"Yeah," said Harold.
"We've spent the last day
traveling through time,
running from dinosaurs,
and teaching cavemen how
to defend themselves!"

"Very funny!" shouted George's dad. "If you kids think you can skip school and goof around all day, you're in for a BIG SURPRISE!"

George and Harold had never seen their parents so angry.

The two boys spent the next five hours mowing lawns, weeding gardens, vacuuming houses, washing cars, dusting furniture, cleaning out garages, whitewashing fences, doing dishes, folding laundry, and taking out garbage. It was exhausting work, but it was nothing compared to what was to come next.

CHAPTER 14
WHAT WAS TO COME NEXT

George and Harold had never been so tired in all their lives. At 9:30 P.M., they grunted "good night" to each other and limped into their houses like zombies.

"Would you like a snack, dear?" said Harold's mother.

"No, thanks," he mumbled. He was too tired for a snack. Too tired to take a bath. Too tired to put his pajamas on or take his shoes off. He didn't even have the energy to turn out his bedroom light. He just collapsed on top of his bed and fell asleep instantly.

Twenty-two seconds later, the telephone rang. It was George.

Harold's mother brought the phone into his room and held it up to his ear. Harold was too tired to even say hello. He just mumbled, "Mmfffff?"

"I just remembered something," said George, panicking. "Tomorrow is *TEST DAY*!!!"

Harold's bloodshot eyes popped open and he sat up straight.

"OH, NO!" Harold cried. "I forgot all about that!"

"Me, too," said George. "We're having major tests in all of our classes tomorrow. We're gonna have to stay up all night long and study!!!"

CHAPTER 15
TO THINE OWN SELF
BE TRUANT

When the sun rose the next day, George and Harold were still going through their spelling checklists. George was almost done studying. Harold still had to read forty-four pages of his natural history textbook.

"Breakfast is ready!" shouted George's dad from downstairs.

George stumbled down exhaustedly and tried to smoosh some waffles into his mouth. He missed.

Meanwhile, Harold was sitting at his
breakfast table in a burned-out stupor,
buttering his cereal and pouring milk on
his toast.

"Did you get *any* sleep at all last night?"
asked Harold's mom.

"OK," Harold answered.

Harold's answer didn't make any sense,
but it was the best he could do under the
circumstances.

Before long, George and Harold were ready for school.

They met up, as they did every school day, in George's front yard.

"Are you ready for all of our big tests today?" asked George droopily.

"Pretty good," said Harold. He was so tired he couldn't even answer a simple question from his best friend correctly. How was he going to manage a day's worth of tests?

"Let's get this over with," George moaned.

"Wait!" said Harold. "I want to check on Crackers's eggs before we go to school."

Harold wobbled to George's backyard
and hoisted himself up the ladder to the
tree house.

"Hurry up!" said George.

Harold did not answer.

"Hey!" shouted George. "We're
gonna be late!"

Harold did not come down.

George climbed up the steps and peeked inside the tree house.

It was just as he had expected. Harold had fallen asleep at their desk.

"Hey, Harold," said George, shaking his friend's shoulder. "Wake up, man! We're gonna be late for our tests!"

"Just five minutes," moaned Harold. "I just need to sleep for five minutes. *PLEASE!!!*"

"Well, OK," said George. "But not a minute longer!"

George took his backpack off and set it against the tree house door. Then he plopped down in his beanbag chair and looked at his pocket watch.

7:53 A.M.

The second hand was ticking by awfully slowly. "I'm just going to close my eyes for a second," said George. "Just for a few seconds . . ."

That afternoon, George yawned and stretched as he rolled over in his beanbag chair. He glanced at his pocket watch again.

4:41 P.M.

George closed his eyes and went back to sleep. Suddenly, his eyes shot open.

"OH! NOOOOO!" George screamed. Harold awoke with a jump. "WE FELL ASLEEP!" George cried. "WE SLEPT THROUGH SCHOOL!!! WE SLEPT THROUGH OUR TESTS!!! WE SLEPT THROUGH EVERYTHING!!!"

"Oh, *NOOO!*" Harold wailed. "We're *DEAD*, man! GAME OVER!!!"

George and Harold peeked out their tree
house window. Harold's mom was out in her
garden. She was whistling a cheerful tune.

"That's strange," said Harold. "Why didn't
the school call her and tell her we were absent?"

"I have no idea," said George.

George and Harold climbed down
from the tree house and walked over to
the garden.

"How was school today?" asked Harold's
mom.

"Oh, same as always, I guess," said
Harold. He really *was* guessing.

George's mom heard them talking and
came over.

"You didn't miss school today, did you?"
asked George's mom.

"Ummm . . . nope," said George.
Technically, George was telling the truth.
He hadn't really *missed* school at all.

CHAPTER 16
SUPER-SECRET TEST DAY

The next day when George and Harold arrived at school, Mr. Krupp was OVERJOYED to see them. He met them at the front door, shook their hands enthusiastically, and gave them both big, sweaty hugs.

"This can't be good," George said.

"You're wrong," said Mr. Krupp. "It's the BEST DAY EVER! It's the day I've been waiting for since I met you two horrible people. Let's all go to my office, shall we? I've got refreshments!"

As they walked down the long hallway toward Mr. Krupp's office, several teachers patted Mr. Krupp on the back and congratulated him. The entire school staff seemed elated.

"We're doomed," said Harold.

When they finally got to Mr. Krupp's office, he plopped down into his chair and spun around a few times, giggling with glee.

After a few minutes, George started to become impatient.

"I thought you said there were going to be refreshments," George said.

"NOT FOR YOU!!!" shouted Mr. Krupp angrily, as he slammed his fist on his desk. He opened his drawer, pulled out a warm diet soda, and popped it open. Then he leaned back in his chair and sipped loudly as he chuckled to himself. "I just want to soak this moment in," he said with delight, as fizzy, brown phosphoric acid dribbled down his chins.

"You boys have REALLY messed up this time." Mr. Krupp laughed. "You skipped school on Super-Secret Test Day!"

"*Super-Secret* Test Day?" said Harold. "What does *that* mean?"

"I thought you'd never ask," Mr. Krupp said gleefully. "You see, I've been looking for a way to separate you two kids for years now, but I never figured out how to do it until yesterday. Then it came to me in a flash of inspiration. SUPER-SECRET TEST DAY!"

"What's so *secret* about it?" asked George.

"You should be asking, 'What's so *SUPER* about it?'" said Mr. Krupp joyfully. "Because it just might be the crowning achievement of my entire career!"

George and Harold looked at each other nervously. Suddenly, the door opened and the school's math teacher, Miss Calculator, entered the room. She sneered down at George and Harold and poked her tongue out at them as she walked by. "Here are the figures you asked for," she said, handing Mr. Krupp a large manila envelope.

"Thanks, Anita," Mr. Krupp said. He smelled the envelope like he was admiring the aroma of a gourmet meal. "It's a real shame you boys missed school yesterday," Mr. Krupp said. "Your teachers *hated* to do it, but they had to give you both *ZEROES* on all of your tests!!!"

"But we studied really hard," said Harold. "Can't we take makeup tests?"

"No, no, no, no, no," Mr. Krupp said, grinning evilly from ear to ear. "There will be no makeup tests!"

"Don't worry, Harold," said George. "We'll do really good on our final exams this year! We can bring our grades back up."

"Final exams have been canceled for this year," said Mr. Krupp cheerfully. "Isn't that wonderful news? You and all your classmates will get seven more weeks of school with no homework, no quizzes, and no studying. Your grades for the whole school year have already been calculated."

"Oh, NO," said George. "We're—we're going to *flunk the fourth grade*?!!?"

"Actually, it's *worse* than that," said Mr. Krupp, his teeth glistening in a grin so wide it seemed to stretch beyond the boundaries of his face. "Normally, you wouldn't get this information until summer vacation begins, but I thought I'd be nice and show you your grades early. Isn't that fun?!!?"

He opened the manila envelope and slid two report cards toward George and Harold. Quickly, the boys opened them up and scanned through them. George's final grade for the year was 62.7 percent. A terrible grade, to be sure, but still a *passing* grade. George would move on to fifth grade next year. Harold, whose grades were not quite as good as George's, wasn't so lucky. Harold's final grade was 59.7 percent. Harold had failed.

"Oh, NO!" Harold moaned, as his eyes began to fill with tears. "I'm going to flunk the fourth grade!"

"Yeah, ain't that too bad?" said Mr. Krupp with a delighted twinkle in his eyes. He looked up at Miss Calculator, and they both burst into fits of laughter.

"There's nothing you can do about it, either," Miss Calculator sneered. "You two brats will be in different grades next year. You'll never see each other in school anymore! You'll have different teachers, different classes . . . and *different friends!*"

CHAPTER 17
THE IDEA

"I can't believe they're going to separate us," said Harold, as the boys walked home from school that afternoon.

George said nothing. He was thinking. He KNEW there was a way to solve this problem.

"I can't believe I have to spend an *EXTRA YEAR* at that school, too," Harold moaned, trying not to cry. "The worst part is that I actually studied! *I know this stuff!* I could have probably gotten *straight Bs* if I had taken those tests yesterday!"

"THAT'S IT!" cried George confidently. "We can fix this!"

"But *HOW*?" said Harold. "They won't let us take makeup tests!"

"Who says we have to take makeup tests?" George replied. "Let's take the *real* tests!"

Harold looked suspicious. "What do you mean?" he asked.

"Melvin said he kept his time-traveling squid thingy in his garage, right?" said George. "Let's borrow it and go back in time to yesterday morning. Then we can take those tests like we were supposed to. Problem solved!"

"No *WAY*!" Harold protested. "Whenever we travel around in time, bad stuff happens!"

"What could be worse than being in different grades next year?" George countered. "Do you really want to spend an extra *YEAR* at that school?"

Harold didn't have an argument for that.

"Besides," said George, "we're only going back in time one day. How could anything bad happen in just one day?"

"I guess you're right," said Harold.

George and Harold turned around and headed over to Melvin's house. Luckily, Melvin's garage door was open. Cautiously, the two boys sneaked inside and looked around. And there, standing in the corner beside a box of Langstrom seven-inch gangly wrenches was the glow-in-the-dark, time-traveling Robo-Squid suit.

"We shouldn't be doing this," Harold whispered. "We're trespassing—and stealing!"

"Hey, Melvin started this whole mess," George reminded Harold. "We're just fixing it! Besides, we're not stealing. We're just *borrowing*."

Against his better judgment, Harold helped hoist George up into the cockpit. Suddenly, the Robo-Squid suit powered up and began to glow. A few moments later, the controls were all set.

"OK," said George. "Let's go back in time and take those dumb tests!" He picked Harold up with one of his glowing tentacles, took a few steps forward, and pressed the "Start" button.

The glow-in-the-dark, time-traveling Robo-Squid suit began shaking and sputtering as it zipped backward in time thirty-two hours. A blinding ball of light flashed suddenly, and George and Harold arrived bright and early yesterday morning, just in time for school.

As Harold helped George climb out of the cockpit, he noticed that there were now *TWO* glow-in-the-dark, time-traveling Robo-Squid suits.

"Hey," said Harold. "How come there are *TWO* glow-in-the-dark, time-traveling Robo-Squid suits?"

"Hmmmm," said George. "I guess that one in the corner is the one from yesterday. When we went back in time, we created a duplicate time machine."

"Oh," said Harold. "Melvin should thank us!"

"Yeah," said George. "That was very thoughtful of us."

George and Harold ran back through town as fast as they could. Soon they were scrambling up the steps of Jerome Horwitz Elementary School.

"This feels weird," said George. "I've never been so happy to go to school before."

"Or to take tests!" said Harold.

And indeed, it was a happy school day for George and Harold. They took all of their tests, did pretty well on most of them, and never had to deal with anything *Super* or *Secret* again. At least not until that afternoon.

CHAPTER 18
OUR DOPPEL GÄNG

That afternoon, when George and Harold got home, they climbed up to their tree house to check on Crackers's eggs. George tried to push the door open, but something was in the way.

"Hey, there's a backpack blocking the door," said George. He reached in and pulled it toward him. "This—this looks like *MY* backpack!"

"What's going on up there?" asked Harold, as George rummaged through the backpack.

"My papers! My books! My lunch from yesterday!" said George. "This *IS* my backpack!"

"It can't be," said Harold. "You're wearing your backpack!"

George pushed the tree house door open and looked inside.

"Oh, *NOOOOO!*" said George.

Harold climbed up next to George and looked inside the tree house. There, sleeping at the table, was Harold himself. And next to him, sprawled out and snoring on his beanbag chair, was George.

"I *TOLD* you something bad would happen!" cried Harold.

"Shhhhh!" said George. "Don't wake us up!"

"I don't understand," Harold whispered. "How come *WE'RE* here?"

"Well, it kind of makes sense," said George. "We just went back in time to yesterday, right?"

"Right," said Harold.

"Well, where were *we* yesterday?" asked George.

"We were right up here in the tree house, sleeping and . . . Oh, I get it," said Harold. "This is us from yesterday!"

"Yeah," said George. "Remember how we accidentally created an extra Robo-Squid suit?"

"Mmm-hmmm," said Harold.

"I guess we accidentally created an extra George and Harold, too."

"Perfect," said Harold sarcastically.

CHAPTER 19
THE PACT

While yesterday's George and Harold slept, George and Harold tried to figure out what to do next.

"How are we going to explain this to our parents?" asked Harold.

"How are we going to explain this to *ourselves*?" asked George.

Yesterday George yawned and stretched as he rolled over in his beanbag chair. He glanced at his pocket watch, then closed his eyes to go back to sleep. Suddenly, his eyes shot open.

"OH! NOOOOO!" Yesterday George screamed. Yesterday Harold awoke with a jump. "WE FELL ASLEEP!" Yesterday George cried. "WE SLEPT THROUGH SCHOOL!!! WE SLEPT THROUGH OUR TESTS!!! WE SLEPT THROUGH—*Hey, who are you guys?*"

Yesterday Harold rubbed his eyes and looked at his twin. "I must be dreaming," he said. "Either that or I'm seeing double!"

"Well," said George, "it's a long story." He and Harold told their yesterday selves what had happened, and quickly caught them both up on the events of the past three and a half chapters.

"*Now* what are we supposed to do?" said Yesterday George.

"We can't tell our parents," said Harold.

"But where are we all going to sleep?" asked Yesterday Harold.

"And how are we all going to get enough food?" said Yesterday George.

"And clean clothes?" said Harold.

Everyone was beginning to panic except for George, who had been deep in thought for a while. George didn't seem worried at all. In fact, a devilish grin was beginning to spread across his face.

"You know," George said, "maybe we're looking at this the wrong way. Maybe this is a *good* thing!"

"A *GOOD* thing?" cried Yesterday Harold incredulously.

"Yeah," said George. "We've always said there's never enough time to do what we *want* to do. So let's take shifts. Me and Harold will start going to school and doing our homework on *even* numbered days, and you guys will go to school and do homework on *odd* numbered days."

"Yeah, but what'll *WE* do while you guys are at school?" asked Yesterday George.

"Whatever you want," said George. "Hang out in the tree house! Play video games! Make comics! Watch monster movies! It doesn't matter. You guys get to relax and take the day off *every other day*!"

"I get it," said Yesterday George, smiling devilishly. "Then YOU guys can take the day off while *WE'RE* at school and stuff."

"Yeah!" said George. "Just think of the possibilities!"

"I don't know," said Harold and Yesterday Harold at the same time.

"Don't worry," said George. "It'll be GREAT! We'll have TWICE as much fun as normal, and only half the work!"

"Yeah!" said Yesterday George. "What could possibly go wrong?"

CHAPTER 20
SHIFT WORKERS

Since today was an even numbered weekday, it was decided that Yesterday George and Yesterday Harold would go to school the next day. So the Yesterday boys said good-bye and headed down to their respective homes to eat, do homework, and prepare for the next day at school.

George and Harold were ready for a night off. Harold grabbed a stack of comics, George turned on a monster movie, and the two friends settled into their beanbag chairs for some well-deserved R and R.

Fortunately, they had enough juice boxes, Zing Zong Cupcakes, and Fruit Rollie-Flops to last them for a while.

Around 9:30 P.M., George called Piqua Pizza Palace and ordered two calzones, some cheesy breadsticks, and two 2-liter bottles of ice-cold root beer.

The boys waited in George's driveway so the delivery guy wouldn't ring the doorbell.

Soon, the two friends were enjoying the finest carbohydrates money could buy, in the quiet comfort of their cozy tree house.

"This is the life," said George, as he pressed "Play" on the horror movie masterpiece *Baby Blob 2: The Squishening*.

Harold, who was usually cautious in situations like this, had to admit it: This was indeed the life.

CHAPTER 21
PROBLEMS

The next morning, George and Harold woke up late. "Ahhh, it's nice to sleep in for a change, isn't it?" said George.

"Yeah," said Harold. "But I gotta pee."

This was something that George and Harold hadn't thought about. Usually, they would just climb down the ladder and run to their houses to use the bathroom. But George's and Harold's moms both worked from home, and they would not be happy to see the boys running in and out of the house on a school day.

Fortunately, empty 2-liter bottles come in very handy for such situations. But as they poured the contents of their emergency urinals out the window, both boys knew this solution wouldn't work for long.

"Our food is running low," said Harold, "and I spent all of my allowance on those calzones last night."

"No problem," said George. "We'll make a comic book, sell it on the playground at school, and use the money to buy all the junk we need! We can even buy one of those portable camping toilet thingies!"

"But we're not supposed to go to school today," said Harold.

"Actually, we're not supposed to go to our classes today!" George clarified. "As long as we're never in the same place as our doubles, we should be fine."

So George and Harold cleared a space at their desk and began working on their newest comic book. It was called:

One morning at the Hoskinses House...

Everybody was watching T.V.

when suddinly...

we interupt this show for Breaking news.

Petey the cat has exscaped from cat jail!

and He has vowed revenge on Super Diaper Baby and Diaper Dog.

Thats terribel!!!

I know!

WE'VE GOT TO BE VERY CARE-FULL!!!

PETEY is going to try and TRICK US!

we must be on the LOOKOUT for his evil ways!

2 Seconds Later...

DING DONG!

OH! I wonder who that could be?

Yes?

HELLO! I'm P.T. Duckhat.

But Then...

Is everyone having fun?

P.T. DuckHat

Yeah!

Good! Because I have one last suprise!!!

He took off his nose...

POP

He took off his makeup...

RUB RUB

He took off his wig and hat...

and he took off his clothes.

Guess who?

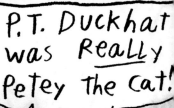

P.T. Duckhat was REALLY Petey the Cat!

get it?

Rar!

OUR HEROS were stuck in the power FULL Grip...

OF the MiGHTY Robo-Baby!

PETEY COLLECTED WaLLets and PURSes FRom the CROWD.

FiLL 'er UP!!!!

Loot

WHILE ROBO BABY DESTROYED The city.

Rar!

Rats! who will Save us?

cheep

Then Dog man got a idea.

He ran over to ROBO-Baby...

and climbed up him.

Then DOG man scrached and scrached.

and scrached!

soon, Dog mans
Fleas flew off.

and They
Landed in
RoBo-BABY's
Diaper.

Then...

I'm
free!

me too!

TRIPLE
FLiP-O-RAMA

FLip it ---
don't Rip
it !!!

Left
Hand HE

DOG Man
had a
Little
itch.

His Fleas
were
white as
Snow.

and every-
where the
ROBO-BABY
Went....

Right
Thum
Here.

DOG MAN had a Little itch.

His Fleas were white as snow.

and everywhere the ROBO-BABY went....

The FLeas were shure to go!

BYe BYe

CAT JAIL

THE END

But Then...

CLICK

TO Be CONTINUED

CHAPTER 23
DREAM A LITTLE DREAM OF US

"Hey, that comic turned out pretty good," said Harold.

"Yeah, not too shabby!" said George. "Let's go to school and make copies of it."

"But what if somebody sees us?" said Harold.

"Don't worry," said George. "I've got it all figured out!"

So George and Harold got dressed, headed to school, and sneaked into the office. In no time at all, they were running off copies of their new comic book and stapling them together. Things were going very well until the school secretary, Miss Anthrope, came back from her lunch break.

"What are you kids doing in my office?!!?" Miss Anthrope yelled.

"We're *not* in your office," said George with a mischievous smile. "You're dreaming!"

"Dreaming?" said Miss Anthrope.

"Yeah! And I can prove it," said George. "Just call our teacher, Ms. Ribble, on the intercom. She'll tell you that we're both in class right now."

"In *class*?" said Miss Anthrope.

"Yep," said George. "Obviously, we can't be in two places at the same time, so this *HAS* to be a dream, right?"

COPYMATIC 2000

Miss Anthrope was suspicious. She grabbed the microphone on the intercom and contacted Ms. Ribble's room.

"Ms. Ribble?" she said. "Where are George and Harold right now?"

"Why, they're right here in my classroom," Ms. Ribble replied through the speaker.

"Oh, *REALLY*?" said Miss Anthrope.

"Of course," said Ms. Ribble. "They've been here all day."

Miss Anthrope was stumped. Then she got a sneaky idea. "Alright," she said. "If they're *really* in your classroom, then send them both to the office right now!"

"OK," said Ms. Ribble.

Miss Anthrope turned and looked at George and Harold with a snarly grin. "I don't know what kind of trick you kids are trying to pull," she said, "but you can't fool me!"

Suddenly, Yesterday George and
Yesterday Harold walked into the office.
Miss Anthrope looked at them and screamed.
Then she looked at George and Harold and
screamed again. Her head made a swishing
sound as it swiveled back and forth between
George and Harold, and Yesterday George
and Yesterday Harold.

"See?" said George. "I *told* you this was
a dream."

"You're—you're *RIGHT*!" cried Miss
Anthrope. "It all seems so vivid! But I
MUST be dreaming!"

"Of course you are," said George. "And
why should you waste a perfectly good
dream hanging around the office?"

"That's a good point!" said Miss Anthrope.
"And why bother wearing such tight,
restricting clothes? After all, it's MY DREAM!
I can do whatever I want!"

"Now, wait a minute," said Harold.

But it was too late. Miss Anthrope hoisted
her dress over her head, ripped it off, and
threw it out the window.

"Wheeeeee!" she yelled. "Dreaming is
FUN!" Then she ran away laughing her head
off and slammed the office door behind her.

"*What are you guys doing here?!!?*" said
Yesterday George sternly. "This is *OUR* day to
be at school!"

"We ran out of food, and we needed to buy
some supplies," said George. "So we made a
new comic to sell on the playground."

Yesterday Harold walked over to the copy machine and inspected the new comic. "How many did you make?" he asked.

"About two hundred," said Harold.

"Well, leave them with us," said Yesterday Harold. "We'll sell them at recess today and bring the money to the tree house after school."

"Yeah," said George. "But we—"

"You guys need to get out of here!" Yesterday George interrupted. "If anybody else catches us together, we'll ALL be in BIG TROUBLE!"

"Alright, alright," said George.

"GET OUT, *NOW*!" shouted Yesterday George angrily.

"ALRIGHT!" said George. *"Gee whiz!"*

Yesterday George and Yesterday Harold scooped up the comics in their arms and left the office in a huff.

"Man," said George. "Today was supposed to be *our* day to have fun! But we won't let us!"

"I know," said Harold. "Who do we think we are?"

"We can't tell us what to do!" said George. "I'm not the boss of me!"

"Me, neither," said Harold. "I'm going to do what I want, even if I don't want me to!"

"That's tellin' yourself!" said George.

CHAPTER 24
TWIN PRANKS

George and Harold went out into the hallway and started switching the letters around on a bulletin board.

Soon they were spotted by two teachers.

"Hey!" Mr. Meaner barked. "What do you kids think you're doing?"

"Actually, we're not doing anything," said George. "You guys are dreaming!"

It took even less effort to persuade Mr. Meaner and Miss Labler that *they* were dreaming, too. Once they looked through Ms. Ribble's classroom window and saw Yesterday George and Yesterday Harold sitting in their seats, they were convinced.

"There can't be TWO Georges and TWO Harolds!" cried Mr. Meaner. "So this *HAS* to be a dream!"

"That's right," said Harold. "You can do ANYTHING you want! Just don't take off your clothes and—"

"Oops, too late."

Mr. Meaner tore off down the hallway
laughing like a crazy person and singing "Itsy
Bitsy Spider" at the top of his lungs. Miss
Labler headed straight for the teachers' lounge,
where she yanked open the refrigerator and
started stuffing her face with everyone's lunches.

"*HALLELUJAH!*" she cried. "I can eat anything
I want and not gain weight!"

"Hey! That's *OUR* food!" cried Mr. Rected.

"No, it's not," giggled Miss Labler. "This is
a dream! Check it out for yourselves!"

With a mouth full of tuna salad and chocolate chip cookies, she led them all down to Ms. Ribble's classroom window. Soon they were convinced, too.

George and Harold watched in shock as
teacher after teacher started going crazy. Mr.
Meaner brought in a garden hose and started
spraying down the hallway with soapy water.
"IT'S THE WORLD'S BIGGEST SLIP 'N'
SLIDE!" he cried.

By the time Mr. Krupp came out of the teachers' bathroom, nearly all of the staff, including the janitor, the lunch ladies, and most of the parent volunteers, were laughing their heads off, throwing soap suds at each other and slipping and sliding down the hallway in their giant underwear.

"WHAT THE HECK IS GOING ON HERE?!!?" Mr. Krupp screamed.

"It's the greatest dream ever!" cried Ms. Dayken.

She brought Mr. Krupp over to Ms.
Ribble's classroom window and showed him
the proof. But when Mr. Krupp saw that
there were now *two* Georges and *two*
Harolds, his reaction was a bit different from
the other adults' reactions. He tried to speak.
He tried to convince himself that he was
dreaming. He tried to say SOMETHING . . .
but all that came out was "B-B-Bubba bobba
hob-hobba-hobba wah-wah."

CHAPTER 25
TWELVE DAYS OF CHAOS

It didn't take long before the cops showed up. They attempted to restore order, but things didn't go very well.

"We can either do this the easy way, or the hard way!" shouted Officer McWiggly.

"Let's do it the *FUN* way!" cried Miss Fitt, as she yanked Officer McWiggly's pants down around his ankles.

"I've got a good idea," said George.

"What?" asked Harold.

"*RUN!*" said George.

By the time it was all over, the entire staff of Jerome Horwitz Elementary School was in jail.

The charges ranged from indecent exposure and resisting arrest to reckless endangerment and *pantsing* a police officer.

The cops didn't quite know what to do with Mr. Krupp, though. He hadn't really done anything wrong. He'd just stood there in the same spot for hours and hours, saying "B-B-Bubba bobba hob-hobba-hobba wah-wah" over and over and *OVER* again.

So it was decided that he should be admitted into the Piqua Valley Home for the Reality-Challenged, where he remained, unchanged, for nearly two weeks.

George and Harold and their twins spent the next twelve days being *VERY* careful.

"Great job!" shouted Yesterday George angrily. "Our teachers are in jail, and Mr. Krupp is in the goof house. These past two weeks have been a total disaster!"

"Two weeks?" said Harold inquisitively.

"Yeah," Yesterday George continued. "In the past two weeks you guys have—"

"No, wait," Harold interrupted. "Wasn't something *BAD* supposed to happen in two weeks?"

George, Yesterday George, and Yesterday Harold all thought back to Melvin Sneedly's cryptic warning in chapter 11.

"Oh, yeah," they all said simultaneously.

The four boys looked around them. They checked the horizon. They sniffed the air. They put their ears to the floor and listened. Nothing. There was no sign of any trouble.

"Huh!" said George. "I guess nothing bad is going to happen after all!"

Suddenly, a fireball shot out from
behind the clouds. Then came an echoing,
eardrum-piercing sound of relentless terror.
It was a laugh. A horrifying, sinister,
stomach-churning laugh that the boys had
not heard for many months. A laugh that
they'd hoped they would never hear again.

"Uh-oh," said the Georges.

"We're doomed!" cried the Harolds.

CHAPTER 26
HEEEEEEEERE'S JOHNNY!

The Turbo Toilet 2000 zipped across the rooftops in his homemade rocket scooter, laughing ferociously as a trail of choking smoke filled the afternoon sky.

Everyone screamed. Everyone cried. Everyone hid.

Everyone, that is, except for George and Harold and their dreadfully distressed duplicates.

The four boys ran as fast as they could to the Piqua Valley Home for the Reality-Challenged.

There was only one person who could stop this horrifying beast, and he was locked away in the goof house.

The four boys dashed through the sanitarium's front door and slid across the freshly waxed floor to the reception desk.

"We need to see Mr. Krupp," cried George, almost out of breath. "He's a patient here."

"Sorry," said the nurse. "But patients can't have visitors without a doctor's permission."

"But he can save the world," cried Harold. "He's Captain Underpants!"

"*Sure he is,*" said the nurse sarcastically. "Listen, bub: We currently have *nine* patients who claim to be Captain Underpants. We also have four Wonder Women, seven Albert Einsteins, and one Elvis Presley!"

"Well, can we at least talk to him?" asked Yesterday Harold.

"No!" said the nurse. "Nobody talks to *The King.*"

"*NOT ELVIS,*" said George angrily. "MR. KRUPP!"

"Oh," said the nurse. "I'm sorry. But *NO!*"

"Rats," cried Yesterday Harold. "Captain Underpants is stuck in the goof house!"

"*We* can't bust him out," said George, "but I know somebody who CAN. Follow me!" Frantically, the boys ran back across the city.

CHAPTER 27
DISGUISE CRAZY!

George had an idea, and he needed everyone's help to pull it off.

Harold grabbed some cardboard boxes from his garage. George found some white spray paint in his garage. Yesterday George and Yesterday Harold each grabbed a barbecue grill from their backyards.

With a little ingenuity and a lot of
duct tape, the four boys constructed two
surprisingly convincing Talking Toilet
costumes.

George and Harold climbed into the boxes and wheeled themselves awkwardly into town. Soon they came face-to-face with the Turbo Toilet 2000.

"Uh, yum, yum, eat 'em up," said George, opening and closing the barbecue grill lid with every syllable.

"Yeah, eat 'em up and stuff," said Harold, doing the same thing with his lid.

"Hey," cried the Turbo Toilet 2000. "I thought you guys were *dead*!"

"I'm not *quite* dead," said George. "It's just a flush wound."

"Yeah, me, too," said Harold.

"Good!" said the Turbo Toilet 2000. "You can help me look for those two kids who messed up all of our plans a few months ago."

"Um, OK," said George. "But what about that bald guy with the cape and the underwear?"

"I'll get him later!" said the Turbo Toilet 2000. "First I want to find those two meddling kids!"

"I really think you should find that underwear guy first," said Harold.

"Yeah," said George. "He said some really mean things about you."

"OH, HE DID, DID HE?" shouted the Turbo Toilet 2000. "What did he say?!!?"

"Ummm . . ." said George. "He said your head is so big, when it rains your body stays dry!"

"Yeah," said Harold, "and you're so cheap, you tried to conserve toilet paper by using both sides."

"ENOUGH!" screamed the Turbo Toilet 2000. "WHERE IS HE?!!?"

"Right this way," said Harold.

CHAPTER 28
ONE SMASHED INTO THE CUCKOO'S NEST

The Turbo Toilet 2000 followed George and Harold back to the sanitarium. He marched through the front doors and headed toward the restricted area. The nurses screamed and ran for safety.

Quickly, George grabbed the intercom, turned up the volume, and started snapping his fingers into the microphone.

The sounds of finger snapping echoed through the hallways of the Piqua Valley Home for the Reality-Challenged as the Turbo Toilet 2000 crashed from room to room. Mr. Krupp, who had been comatose for nearly two weeks, suddenly began to change. First, a mischievous twinkle gleamed in his eyes. Then a giant smile spread across his face. Suddenly, he ripped off his straitjacket, threw off his pajamas, and grabbed a curtain from a nearby window.

Captain Underpants was back, and the
battle of the century was about to begin.

CHAPTER 29
THE INCREDIBLY GRAPHIC VIOLENCE CHAPTER, PART 2 (IN FLIP-O-RAMA™)

FLIP-O-RAMA 4

(pages 177 and 179)

Remember, flip *only* page 177.
While you are flipping, be sure you
can see the picture on page 177
and the one on page 179.
If you flip quickly, the two
pictures will start to look like
<u>one</u> *animated* picture.

Don't forget to
add your own sound-effects!

LEFT HAND HERE

WELCOME TO
POUND TOWN!

RIGHT
THUMB
HERE

RIGHT
INDEX
FINGER
HERE

178

WELCOME TO POUND TOWN!

FLIP-O-RAMA 5

(pages 181 and 183)

Remember, flip *only* page 181.
While you are flipping, be sure you
can see the picture on page 181
and the one on page 183.
If you flip quickly, the two
pictures will start to look like
<u>one</u> *animated* picture.

Don't forget to
add your own sound-effects!

LEFT HAND HERE

SPANK YOU VERY MUCH!

RIGHT
THUMB
HERE

RIGHT
INDEX
FINGER
HERE

182

SPANK YOU
VERY MUCH!

FLIP-O-RAMA 6

(pages 185 and 187)

Remember, flip *only* page 185.
While you are flipping, be sure you
can see the picture on page 185
and the one on page 187.
If you flip quickly, the two
pictures will start to look like
<u>one</u> *animated* picture.

Don't forget to
add your own sound-effects!

LEFT HAND HERE

ALL'S SWELL
THAT ENDS SWELL!

RIGHT
THUMB
HERE

RIGHT
INDEX
FINGER
HERE

186

ALL'S SWELL
THAT ENDS SWELL!

CHAPTER 30
TEARS OF A COMMODE

"Let that be a lesson to you," said Captain Underpants gallantly, as the Turbo Toilet 2000 cried and cried.

"Well," said George, "I'm glad that's over with!"

"Yeah," said Harold. "That ended up being a lot easier than I thought it would be!"

At that precise moment, a single teardrop from the quivering eyeballs of the Turbo Toilet 2000 flew through the air and landed on Captain Underpants's face. *Splash!* Suddenly, our hero's expression began to change. The sparkle disappeared from his eyes, his posture deflated, and his goofy grin morphed into a scowling grimace.

"What the heck is going on here?!!?" Mr. Krupp yelled.

"Uh-oh," said Harold.

Mr. Krupp turned and saw the ginormous
Turbo Toilet 2000 blubbering behind him.
"AAAAAUGH!" the frightened principal
shrieked. "IT'S A MONSTER!!!" And he ran
away, screaming his head off.

The Turbo Toilet 2000 wasn't sure what was going on, but he decided to chase Mr. Krupp and see what happened. Soon, the leviathan lavatory cornered Mr. Krupp and scooped him up in his mighty robotic fist.

"I give up!" cried Mr. Krupp. "I surrender! Please don't hurt me!"

"Gee," said the Turbo Toilet 2000. "That ended up being a lot easier than I thought it would be! Now I just need to find those two annoying kids!"

Mr. Krupp perked up a little. "Er, what two annoying kids?" he asked.

"Well," said the Turbo Toilet 2000, "one of them had a flat-top and a tie, and the other one wore a T-shirt and had a bad haircut!"

"Hey, I know those kids!" said Mr. Krupp excitedly. "I even know where they live!"

"Really?" said the Turbo Toilet 2000. "Then what are we waiting for? Come on, my two toilet minions. Behold, my tyrannical retaliation is at hand!"

Mr. Krupp pointed the way, and the Turbo Toilet 2000 marched off toward George's and Harold's houses.

"Uh-oh," said George.

"We're doomed again," said Harold.

CHAPTER 31
THE RE-RETALIATION

The Turbo Toilet 2000 marched to George's and Harold's houses, smashing through buildings, pushing over cars, and leaving a smoldering path of destruction behind him. George and Harold tried to keep up, but the Turbo Toilet 2000 left them trailing behind.

"Oh, NO!" cried Harold. "He's heading for our houses, and there's no way to warn ourselves!"

It didn't matter, however, because
Yesterday George and Yesterday Harold
could hear the Turbo Toilet 2000 coming
from miles away.

"I think he's heading straight for us,"
cried Yesterday George.

"But how would he know where to find
us?" asked Yesterday Harold.

"Turn left at Vine Street," said Mr. Krupp.
"The kids live on this block. I'll bet they're
hiding up in that tree house of theirs!"

Yesterday George and Yesterday Harold
saw the Turbo Toilet 2000 heading for their
backyard. They could feel the Earth shake
under each stomp of his massive, metal feet.
Yesterday George locked the door to the tree
house. Yesterday Harold hid under the desk.

195

"OK," said Mr. Krupp. "I've led you to those two kids you were looking for. Can I go now?"

"Sure," said the Turbo Toilet 2000. "You can go *right in here*!" He shoved the screaming principal into his mouth and flushed his little handle. Mr. Krupp shrieked in terror as he spun around in a swirling whirlpool of saliva. Then the Turbo Toilet 2000 swallowed hard, and Mr. Krupp was flushed away with a gurgling *glug, glug, glug*.

The Turbo Toilet 2000 slammed against
the tree with his massive, metallic shoulder.
Yesterday George and Yesterday Harold
went flying. The bookshelf fell over, comics
flew everywhere, and Crackers's eggs wobbled
around precariously on the desktop.

"GET DOWN HERE, YOU MEDDLING KIDS!" screamed the Turbo Toilet 2000, as he smashed into the tree once more. Yesterday George and Yesterday Harold went flying again. The three eggs teetered perilously back and forth at the edge of the table.

"I'M WARNING YOU!!!" cried the Turbo
Toilet 2000. "GIVE UP NOW AND I WON'T
MAKE YOU SUFFER!" He plowed into the
tree a third time. This time, the window
smashed, the TV toppled over, and Crackers's
eggs flew off of the table.

Yesterday George and Yesterday Harold leaped for the eggs.

"NOOOOOOOO!" cried Yesterday Harold, as the three purple-and-orange-speckled eggs flew through the air. They hit the floor and shattered with a terrible crash.

CHAPTER 32
SURPRISE, SURPRISE, SURPRISE!

As the tree house swayed violently from side to side, Yesterday George and Yesterday Harold sifted frantically through the broken eggshell fragments. Suddenly, Yesterday Harold's hand felt something warm and fuzzy. Carefully, he pulled it out of the broken eggshell pieces.

It was a . . . a . . . Yesterday Harold wasn't quite sure *what* it was.

"What the heck is this thing?" cried Yesterday Harold, as the tiny fuzzy creature wrapped its wings around him and looked up lovingly into his eyes.

Yesterday George pulled two more fuzzy winged creatures out of the shell fragments and stared at them in disbelief.

"This—*this can't be*," he cried.

The tree house shook wildly, and Yesterday George and Yesterday Harold went flying again. The three tiny creatures happily wiggled their way up to the boys' faces and started licking their cheeks.

The Turbo Toilet 2000 climbed up the side
of the tree and tore the door off its hinges. He
reached in and grabbed Yesterday George and
Yesterday Harold in his mighty, metallic hand.

"I'VE GOT YOU NOW!" roared the
preposterous porcelain predator, as he shook
the two boys back and forth. The three fuzzy
creatures fell to the floor. Quickly, they got to
their feet and excitedly flapped their wings.
They weren't sure what was happening, but it
seemed like fun.

The Turbo Toilet 2000 jumped down from the tree house and squeezed the two boys tightly in his fist.

"Finally, I shall avenge my fallen allies and take my place as the SUPREME LEADER OF THE EARTH!" he shouted.

The three tiny creatures fluttered down to Yesterday George and Yesterday Harold, wagging their little tails with excitement. But when they saw the looks of terror on the boys' faces, they realized that this was not a game.

Quickly, the three creatures took action
and began circling the Turbo Toilet 2000 like
mosquitoes. Then they each took turns
zooming in close and taking quick bites out
of him with their bionic jaws.

"OUCH!" cried the Turbo Toilet 2000, as he
desperately swatted at the swooping creatures.
"What the heck ARE those things?"

Another one dived in, bit him on the forearm, and yanked out a steel bolt.

"HEY! CUT THAT OUT!" screamed the frustrated fiend, as he released the boys and began swatting at the flying beasties with all his might.

The strange furry creatures grasped the Turbo Toilet 2000 by his lid and shoulders and lifted him off the ground. Flapping their wings as hard as they could, they carried the villainous lavatory higher and higher into the air.

LEFT HAND HERE

IT'S MY POTTY
AND I'LL FLY
IF I WANT TO.

RIGHT
THUMB
HERE

RIGHT
INDEX
FINGER
HERE

210

IT'S MY POTTY
AND I'LL FLY
IF I WANT TO.

Soon they were more than a half mile up in the sky.

"LEMME GO! LEMME GO!" roared the terrified Turbo Toilet 2000. This turned out to be a poor choice of words, because the three fuzzy creatures did exactly that.

All at once, they released their grip on the evil, robotic behemoth, and sent him tumbling downward. Faster and faster he fell through the clouds, spinning out of control and screaming in terror.

CHAPTER 34
WELCOME BACK, KRUPP

The Turbo Toilet 2000 had smashed into a
vacant parking lot and exploded with a sonic
boom that shattered nearly every window in
the city.

When the smoke finally cleared, Mr. Krupp
sat alone in the center of the impact point,
surrounded by mangled metal and jagged
chunks of porcelain. Everything around him
had been destroyed, but Mr. Krupp, surprisingly,
was unharmed. His super powers had
protected him.

Soon, two cops arrived at the scene. "Are you OK?" they asked.

"I guess so," said Mr. Krupp. "This must be one of those crazy nightmares I keep having!"

"Oh, *great*!" said Officer McWiggly. "It looks like we've got another naked schoolteacher who thinks he's *dreaming*!"

"Let's lock him up with the others," said the chief of police.

CHAPTER 35
HAMSTERDACTYLS

George and Harold finally made it home just
as the three furry creatures were returning
to the tree house. Yesterday George and
Yesterday Harold told them what had
happened, and how the strange, fuzzy
creatures inside Crackers's eggs
had saved the Earth from
total destruction.

"What *are* these things anyway?" asked George.

"They kinda look like a cross between a hamster and a pterodactyl," said Harold.

"Eewww!" said George. "That means that Sulu and Crackers w-w-were—EEEWWWW!"

"But that doesn't make sense," said Harold. "How could a mammal mate with a reptile?"

"EEEEWWWWW!" cried George again.

"I mean, unless Sulu's DNA was mutated when he morphed with that bionic endoskeleton," said Harold.

"EEEEEWWWWWW!" cried George again.

"I suppose a mammal with mutated genes *MIGHT* be able to breed with a prehistoric reptile," Harold speculated.

"What part of *EEEEEEWWWWWWW* don't you understand?!!?" shouted George.

"Sorry," said Harold.

Soon, the four friends and their three new
pets were back up in their tree house. They
all worked together to clean up the mess.
Then the two Harolds made beds for the baby
hamsterdactyls out of shoe boxes, while the
two Georges thought up names for them.

"Let's call the girl *Dawn*," said George.

"What about the two boys?" asked Yesterday
Harold.

"*Orlando* and *Tony*," said Yesterday George.

Harold wrote their new pets' names
on their shoe box beds, but he still seemed
perplexed.

"Are you *still* trying to figure out how
we ended up with three half-pterodactyl,
half-bionic-hamster pets?" asked George.

"Yeah, sort of," Harold replied.

"You're thinking too much," said George.
"Listen, if you look too closely at these
stories, they're gonna fall apart completely.
Whaddya think this is, *Shakespeare*?!!?"

"I guess you're right," said Harold.

"Of course I'm right," said George. "Just
go with it, man."

CHAPTER 36
ALL'S WELL
THAT ENDS POORLY

"Well, that was a satisfying ending," said
Yesterday Harold, as he tucked Tony, Orlando,
and Dawn into their beds.

"What do you mean, *satisfying*?" said
George. "The city is destroyed, our teachers
are in jail, there are *four* of us, and our three
mutant pets think we're their *moms*!"

"Oh, yeah," said Yesterday Harold. "I guess
there *are* a lot of loose ends in this story."

"Uh-oh," said Harold. "That
can only mean one thing!"

"What?" asked
Yesterday George.

Dawn   Orlando   Tony

"Another SEQUEL!!!" said Harold.
"OH, NO!" whined George and Yesterday George.
"Here we go again!!!" moaned Harold and Yesterday Harold.

GET READING WITH DAV PILKEY!

ABOUT THE
AUTHOR-ILLUSTRATOR

When Dav Pilkey was a kid, he was diagnosed with ADHD and dyslexia. Dav was so disruptive in class that his teachers made him sit out in the hallway every day. Luckily, Dav loved to draw and make up stories. He spent his time in the hallway creating his own original comic books — the very first adventures of Dog Man and Captain Underpants.

In college, Dav met a teacher who encouraged him to write and illustrate for kids. He took her advice and created his first book, WORLD WAR WON, which won a national competition in 1986. Dav made many other books before being awarded the California Young Reader Medal for DOG BREATH (1994) and the Caldecott Honor for THE PAPERBOY (1996).

In 2002, Dav published his first full-length graphic novel for kids, called THE ADVENTURES OF SUPER DIAPER BABY. It was both a USA Today and New York Times bestseller. Since then, he has published more than a dozen full-length graphic novels for kids, including the bestselling Dog Man and Cat Kid Comic Club series.

Dav's stories are semi-autobiographical and explore universal themes that celebrate friendship, empathy, and the triumph of the good-hearted.

When he is not making books for kids, Dav loves to kayak with his wife in the Pacific Northwest.

Learn more at Pilkey.com.